H.P. Manning
RIDER

Copyright© H.P. Manning, 1999, 2005

All Rights reserved.
COVER ART BY JOHN N. WILBANKS

PUBLISHER'S NOTE

This is a work of fiction, The characers, incidental places, and dialogues areproducts of the author's imagination and are not to be construed as real. The author's use of names of actual persons, living or dead, is incidental to the purposes of the plot and is not intended to change the entirely fictional character of the work.

Rider Publications, Inc.

Manufactured in the United States of Americia.
Set in Adobe Caslon
DESIGNED BY JOHN N. WILBANKS

All rights reserved under International and Pan American Copyright Convention. No part of this book may be reproduced or transmitted in any form or by any means, electronic or mechanical, including photocopying, recording, or by any information storage and retrieval system, without permission in writing from the publisher.

To my sister–in–law *Sandi*.
Thanks for the inspiration.

Chapter One

The rain had come down in torrents for almost twenty minutes before Lucas found the small bridge to park the modified F.X.R.T. under and sit out the worst of the storm. Lucas didn't mind a ride in a reasonable rain, but this was suicide to continue.

He opened the brand new black leather, silver-studded saddlebags that had been the final touch to the new look for his bike. He picked out two of the semi-cold beers, and then settled back on the concrete embankment under the narrow bridge.

The rain continued to drum down. He pondered over his first ride in over two years. It really didn't matter about the rain or the delay. Lucas had dreamed about this trip during the past two years while he was in prison. Time was irrelevant now; he was free, he had done his bit, and the dream of this road trip to see his brother Dave in Florida had helped him through it.

The bike looked a lot different now. Three weeks before Lucas caught his case, he had hit a deer; it had done in the fairing, the windshield, the fiberglass saddlebags, and the trunk. It looked like a Harley now; nobody would ever call it a "Honda-Harley" again. That used to really burn Lucas's ass.

He approached the Harley for another beer, the rain let up, so he decided against the beer and started to put on his rain gear. Lucas knew he would have to be very careful not to screw up his parole. He knew how petty the bureaucracy was; it would be easier to put an ex-con back in than to convict a new one.

The rain had all but quit now, and the sun was bleeding through the clouds. The steam off the highway was like a vapor that wanted to seep back into the clouds.

While fastening the second strap on his new, not-so-shiny saddlebags, a small van pulled off the road under the bridge behind him. From where he was squatting, stowing his rain gear, he watched as a shapely tan leg reached to the ground from the shotgun seat of the van. The late afternoon sun had come out and was directly in his eyes and he was headed eastward out of the mountains of North Carolina to the coast. Lucas stood up; he wanted to see more. He reached into his handle bar pouch for his sunglasses. Now, as he put his glasses on and turned, he saw that the shapely leg belonged to a lovely, dark-haired beauty about thirty years old. Now the driver got out and Lucas saw that she was equally beautiful, if not more so.

The girls were no more than fifteen yards away as they looked at each other, nodded, smiled, and started their approach toward him.

Lucas's heart rate doubled as the delectable duo drew nearer. Lucas had been out of the joint for only two weeks, but he had managed to enjoy himself with two of the girls that used to ride with him from time to time. Nevertheless, his appetite was insatiable for such delicacies since his two years of famine. Now his mind was racing as fast as his heart as the women stopped and smiled at him across the bike.

"Hi," the one who had been riding shotgun said, "Are you having trouble?"

"No," Lucas said, "I just took a break from the rain. I was fixin' to take off when you ladies pulled up."

"Where ya headed to?" the driver asked with a smile that could melt an Eskimo.

Lucas smiled back and wondered where this was going, then said, "I'm cutting across the mountains here to the coast and down to Jax's Beach, Florida, to see my brother. By the way, my name's Lucas," extending his hand over the bike to the girls.

The one that had been riding shotgun quickly reached over, clasping his hand with a firm but gentle grip, and said, "I'm Tess, and this is Terry." He shook the driver's hand.

"Where y'all headed to?" Lucas asked.

Now it was Terry's turn to answer as she moved around to Lucas's side of the bike. "We're going about an hour and a half east of here, the same way you're headed." Lucas was about to say something when Terry said, "I've never ridden on a Harley before. My little brother had a little rice-burner I rode on a few times, but it was nothing like your big ol' Harley there."

Lucas wasn't sure if the girls were putting him on or if they were for real. He looked at both of them with lustful eyes behind the dark glasses and knew his luck had surely taken a right turn.

"Terry," he said, "I've got an extra skid lid if you want to ride with me for a ways."

Terry squealed like a kid and began to jump up and down, clapping her hands.

"Could I, Could I?!" she said.

Lucas zeroed in that when Terry jumped up and down, she wore no bra, and the excitement in her round, firm breasts showed.

Tess now spoke up, saying, "Wait a minute! Only if I get the next ride."

"Oh, Tess, you're such a tease." Terry said.

"Oh, no! Not today," replied Tess.

As they readied themselves to leave, Lucas gazed up at the sky. The girls thought he was looking at the clouds for rain, but Lucas gave quick thanks for his freedom, his luck, and especially, for the delectable duo that had been sent his way.

Terry mounted up with a big smile still on her pretty lips. She hugged closely to Luke with her firm breasts pressed warmly against Lucas's still damp T-shirt. He felt her warmth and his desire was growing; it took great effort on his part to relax and go on.

They rode down the winding, two-lane, mountain road, Tess following behind. Every time Terry wanted to say something, she would lean way forward and press her warm body hard against Lucas. He told her that he was hungry; she said she knew of a nice little restaurant with good food for a cheap price about thirty or forty miles down the road.

They rode on with little talk. Terry would occasionally wave back to Tess, who kept a safe distance behind. Once, Lucas turned to comment on how pretty the view was; then he let his hand slide along Terry's smooth leg. She quickly put her hand over his and held it there for a long time. When she finally did move her hand from his, he gave her leg a little pat, and she hugged close to him, rubbing her hands over his chest in a smooth, seductive motion.

When they topped the mountain, Terry pointed ahead to the right where a sign hung in front of an old, long, log building. Lucas slowed and geared down. Terry signed to Tess and she followed their lead. Lucas slowed down almost to a stop before he entered the graveled parking lot; the last thing he wanted to do was dump this lovely creature in the gravel and wake up from this beautiful dream.

Lucas held the bike steady while Terry climbed off. She pulled off her helmet, threw her arms around

Lucas's neck, and gave him a big, wet kiss. Then she ran over to the van where Tess stood. The two girls conversed for a few minutes, and then joined Lucas. Each grabbed an arm and Tess leaned over and kissed Lucas on the cheek.

"It's my turn now, baby," Tess said as the three of them with linked arms climbed up the steps to the café.

The waitress called the delectable duo by name as she saw them to a table.

Tess sat close to Lucas in the booth and put her hand on his leg. He reached down and gently squeezed her hand; she smiled and softly rubbed his leg.

Their orders came, the food was good, and the conversation was smooth and easy. Lucas learned that they were, indeed, sisters as he had expected. They told him of a bar out in the country that really rocked on Friday nights, and it was Friday.

Lucas told the girls that he didn't like to drink more than two or three beers and ride. The girls quickly told him that there was no need to. Their cabin was only a few miles from the bar and they had plenty of room for him. He smiled at both of them and gave Tess a little hug.

On the ride to the cabin, Tess rode with Luke and snuggled close to him. She also wore no bra, and, like Terry, she pressed her nicely proportioned breasts against his back.

They pulled up to the house, and Tess jumped off the second the bike stopped. She ran with high, springy jumps to the van as Terry pulled up. She said a few words to Terry, and then ran back to Lucas, throwing herself on him with her arms widespread. She grabbed around his neck, and they both went down. She planted a big, wet kiss on him and said, "Welcome home, Luke!"

The girls went in to shower and change. Lucas said he would rest up out on the front porch. He sat and drank a few beers, and his thoughts were on his good fortune; without a doubt, his luck had changed.

The bar was jumpin' when they arrived; a southern rock band was playing "Freebird." Terry swept Lucas straight to the dance floor; Tess said she would grab a table.

The night went on with drinks, dance, laughter, and small talk. The people he met were friendly enough. The only thing that bothered him any was that, several times, he saw people that would look at him, and then two or three would turn and talk with an occasional glance in his direction. Lucas figured they had plenty of reason; here he was, a stranger with the two prettiest girls in the place.

At about ten-thirty, Tess and Terry told Lucas that they were ready to go home. They said that they wanted to party alone with Lucas.

What these two girls and Lucas did for the next two and a half hours made the Greek orgies look like amateur hour. It was out of the realm of reality; it surpassed any expectations Lucas had ever had.

Lucas woke up in a fog; his head was like an anvil that hot horseshoes had been pounded on all day. He could barely open his eyes, and no other part of his body would move. He lay still and concentrated so he might regain his senses. His eyes cleared somewhat, and through the small crack of the door opening he could see the flicker of candlelight in the next room. He heard the faint sound of two voices at once, like prayers in unison. He could smell the pungent odor of incense. It brought to mind the memories of his childhood visits to see his aunt in the convent.

He concentrated harder and tried to move, but it was no use. There were shadows moving and more voices joined in the cantor. The door opened all the way now, and what Luke saw sent a wave of shock through his entire nervous system. Tess stood with a single candle; she wore an open, black-hooded robe, exposing her blood smeared, naked body. She moved closer. Lucas closed his eyes and he could feel her warm breath on his sweaty face for a few seconds, then she retreated. She closed the door, she turned and said, "He's still out, we've got plenty of time."

Lucas's concentration turned into prayers; tears came to his eyes and his body began to tremble. He realized that he could move; slowly and painfully, he sat up. He was mad at himself.... what a fool he had been! The perfect victim, he had been drugged, which had been done easily enough.

Pants and shirt finally on, boots in his hand, he slowly tiptoed to the door and peeked through the crack. There were six people in a circle on the floor; all wearing the black robes, and at least two of them were men.

"Witches! Stinking-assed witches!" Lucas exclaimed to himself. They were hungry, and he was the main course. He knew that if he didn't make his move now, he would be taken into the bowels of a dark labyrinth from which there would be no escape.

He knew he could never go over all six of them, and they were right in the path of the door. Quietly, he made his way to the window. He let out a sigh of relief when it opened easily. The screen was a different matter. It was the old, wooden type with twenty years of layered paint on it. Lucas knew he would never get out without being heard. He took out his bike keys, pushed one against the screen, and tested the strength of it. It was tight and very thick.

He backed up to the door; as he did, he heard footsteps right outside the room. Without a thought, he ran at the window and dived with his head down and his fists straight out in front of him. He hit the ground and rolled; as he got to his feet, he heard a big voice say, "Stop, you son-of-a-bitch, or I'll shoot!"

Without a look back, Lucas jumped the Harley like a cowboy, hit the keyhole on the first try, pushed the electric start button and, all in one movement he shot out into the dark. He came around the front of the house, there was a flash from the front porch and the bike swayed, but he bore down even harder.

He rode as if the devil were after him, and, the way Lucas saw it, he was. After a safe distance, feeling sure nobody was on his tail; he pulled over to put on one of the helmets fastened to the brand new, black leather, silver studded saddlebags. Looked down, he saw that the bag was full of holes, like those from a shotgun blast.

Lucas rode east, he smiling, yea his luck had certainly taken a turn.

Chapter Two

After a thirty minute ride, the adrenaline rush had given way to total exhaustion. Lucas was ready to pull off the narrow, two-lane road at any clearing and crash out for what was left of the night.

The thought came to him that he didn't even know where he was. The events and his hasty exit had left him numb, but now the numbness was wearing off and the pain was setting in. He knew two things for sure: he was alive, and he wasn't brain dead.

During his quest for the delectable duo, his direction was completely lost and now his pride was as lost as he was. All of this would be temporary, nonetheless he was pissed. He was regaining his senses as the wind blew pain into the raw places that the screen and the gravel had left. At that moment, the road made a very sharp curve to the right and ended at a T. He had come close to losing it as he slid to a halt.

Harley made a great bike, but even their brakes had to be replaced. He smiled as he thought about the new caliber that he had Duke put on the rear wheel just the day before he had left on this eventful ride.

Now, here he was sitting at this T, no road signs, not even a damn stop sign. He was somewhere in the middle of the mountains of North Carolina. The gentle rumble of the Harley was the only sound of the night besides an annoying song, the old Credence tune, "I Put A Spell On You", running through his head. How appropriate, he thought as he rubbed his face and shook his head.

It had been a fifty-fifty chance which way to turn: left or right. The left turn proved to be the right choice, for just over the next mountain there were lights. Salvation! Maybe a motel where he could lick his wounds and get some sleep.

He pulled into a dimly lit parking lot hitting the kill button. No need to wake everyone in the joint, he thought. His feet touched down and he was letting out a breath of anger, frustration and relief as he was surprised by a voice. "Holy shit," he muttered to himself as every nerve in his body went on alert. Turning to the left, he looked to the direction that the voice had come from, but saw nothing.

"You're out late, Rider," the no-faced voice said. "Room two is open, your bike is fine right where it is. You can pay me when you wake up; it'll be twenty bucks including tax."

Lucas had dismounted and looked over into the shadows of a dim light where the voice had come from. He could tell by the tone that it belonged to an older man. The light didn't allow him to see anything but a silhouette sitting in an old, high back rocker. A door to the right opened and light flooded out giving a clear view of the old man. Hell, he was ancient! You could look into that face and read a story. The time lines were deep and the hair was thick and white. Lucas had never seen anyone that looked as ancient. The old man was the inventor of time itself.

A sweet young voice of concern said from behind the door, "Is it him, Pap Paw?"

"Yes, child, now go back to bed," he replied.

Lucas opened the door to room two. He found the switch and flicked the light on. What the hell had the girl meant, "Is it him"? He found himself getting pissed off all over again. He opened the door with a strong, forcible movement and walked over to his bike, all the while staring in the direction of the ancient one. Lucas unstrapped his bag, using quick, sharp movements of anger. When he turned, the ancient one spoke.

"It's all right, boy, I'll keep an eye on things tonight." His tone took on another dimension than it had earlier. It was strong, but kind. It gave Lucas a little reassurance that he needed at this point.

"Thanks," said Lucas as he got to the door and closed it.

"Just as well," he thought aloud, "I'll be ready." He opened his bag and right on top was his old K-bar. He slid it out of the scabbard, looking at it like an old friend.

Then he slid it back in and put it under the pillow. Enough was enough for one night. He hit the light and undressed in the dark. The cool, clean sheets felt good against his tired and pain wrenched body.

His last thoughts before falling into a deep, dark sleep were of his wounds, and how he needed to shower and clean them.

Lucas awakened to a rustling sound in the room. He sat straight up in bed; his eyes were wide open but fogged from the deep sleep and whatever drugs those two bitches had given him.

His eyes began to clear, his head began to pound so violently that he thought he would pass out. He rolled over to his right side and squeezed his temples with the palms of both hands. He began to focus on what, or who was intruding on his room and sleep, he saw the backside of a very shapely woman with long, streaming blonde hair. It was long and bright, it was as if light was shining from it.

The woman turned and looked over at Lucas. She had the face of an angel and a voice to match. "Sorry to disturb you, but its good that you're finally awake. When you get showered and dressed, my Pap Paw wants you to come around back to the house and eat. We'll talk then," she said. The door opened, letting in the dim light of day and she was gone in one quick flowing motion.

Lucas knew that he had died and gone to heaven. She was no doubt an angel. She was everything he had ever envisioned an angel to look and be like. He began to move to the side of the bed when the pain hit him. He knew then that was very much alive! Lucas had been told since he was a little boy that heaven was a beautiful place with no pain of any kind. "Oh, shit," he moaned, "I knew it was too good to be true. I'm still alive."

He got out of bed slowly. The lower part of his back ached and his kidneys hurt, but most of that was due to his long absence from riding.

The scrapes on his right knee, his elbows, and the palm of his left hand were sore, but they looked like old wounds, maybe a week or ten days old. This is strange, he thought as he examined himself.

He turned around and looked at the bed where he had been laying. The sheets were stained with dark brown, dried blood. He could feel the tightness of the skin on his back where the screen had tore at him during his frantic escape; but there was no real pain.

Talking to himself as he moved toward the sink and mirror he said, "What the hell is going on here?" He looked up on the small, old oak chest and discovered his jeans and socks were freshly washed and folded. A new black tee shirt sat next to them. The shirt had a picture of the mountains and the words North Carolina across the top and written across the bottom was the single word: Serenity. Serenity my stinking ass, Lucas muttered to himself. This is turning into a damned nightmare. He rubbed the palm of his left hand and found an oily substance on it. He brought it up to his nose, smelled, and quickly jerked it away. "Holy Shit!" Lucas cried out, "These crazy ass hillbillies have wiped a skunk's ass on me while I slept." He turned to look in the mirror. His head shot to the right as if the left side had been struck with a baseball bat. He got up closer to the mirror. Slowly, with his index finger and thumb, he pulled and separated a half inch wide and three inch long gray streak of hair at his left temple, and gently pulled it to the side of his head.

"Oh shit, shit, shit! Sweet mamma of Moses! What the hell is happening to me?" Lucas screamed. "Maybe it was that damned skunk they used; the damned white streak went left and missed center. Holy shit! All the hell I want to do is get the hell out of these mountains and away from these crazy ass mountain people. Serenity my ass!"

Lucas had a bad habit of talking to his self, even to the extent of having a full-blown argument.. He jumped into the shower. He knew how he must have needed it after having a skunk's ass wiped all over him.

The shower was soothing and relaxed his tension and his temper. Soon his thoughts had drifted toward the beautiful angel that had been in his room just minutes before.

Oh no, dumb ass, he thought. That is what got you into this shape to begin with, letting that damned little head do the thinking for you. He would pay them, thank them for their kindness and jump his little ass on his Harley and ride south. He would ride hard and fast and never look back. The shower proved to do the trick. Lucas felt as if it was a shower of baptism and had washed away his sins of the past few days. The feeling was short lived, however, for when he stepped in front of the mirror he still looked like shit. The new streak of gray hair would stand as a reminder of how easy it had been for those two beauties to con him. He could feel his blood getting hot; his temples began to pound. He leaned over the sink just inches away from the mirror. Looking directly into his own eyes, what he saw scared him. Lucas had not seen that fire in his eyes since Vietnam.

While he shaved and readied himself to hit the road, it hit him how hungry he was. "Yeah, I'll go around back to the house and eat. There's no need to be rude. After all, these people have gone out of their way to help me."

"Talking to himself he looked into the mirror and pointed, "Okay, rubber head, that's as good as it gets for you today. Yeah, eat, be polite and get the hell out of all this crazy shit."

He stepped out into the cool evening air, and realized "Cool evening air? Holy shit! I slept all day! I had my mouth all set to eat some good ole biscuits and gravy, bacon and eggs; shit! Now I'll probably have to eat stewed skunk with shit gravy on the side. Oh, yeah; I'm having a big time now."

Passing through a narrow hallway and going by the small office Lucas saw a sign on the door that read "Ring Bell For Service". He had to smile, thinking how laid back these people are. He walked by an old Lance vending machine and a R.C. Cola box; they were both dingy and faded. He hadn't seen machines like these since he was a kid growing up in west Tennessee. At the end of the hallway, off to the right was a cobblestone path. To the left of the path was a twenty-foot drop-off with layers of broken, jagged rocks on both sides. At the bottom ran a crystal clear stream. It ran about two or three feet deep. He had been in a few of these mountain streams before and, by God, they were cold.

At the end of the short path, to his left stood an old footbridge. It was the only apparent way to get across the narrow gorge.

Taking his time and absorbing the serene beauty of this timeless space he had passed into, a voice interrupted his state of tranquility that he had allowed himself to slip into.

"Hey, rider, watch your step. Those damned stairs are steeper than they look." Lucas shook off his trance. He bent his head straight back, gleaming up the steep rock steps that led to the porch of the mystical old man's domain.

What a sight the old man was up there on his porch. His long, white hair flowed back over his shoulders as a gentle, cool breeze blew. He was taller than Lucas had first thought him to be, but the only time Lucas had seen him he had been sitting down and it had been dark.

Lucas climbed the rock stairway, he was observing the Ancient One with great intensity. At the same time he could feel that he was being sized up himself.

When he reached the porch he extended his hand out in greeting; the Ancient One moved closer. His movement was quick and direct, unlike that of an old man. He caught Lucas's extended hand with his extra large hand and firmly shook it while his other hand quickly grasped Lucas's shoulder for a warm greeting. Even though the Ancient One was old and bent, Lucas could see that he had once been a powerful man. From the large, oversized hands to the big, square shoulders and a jaw that was square and firm, this was a man of definite action and few words.

Lucas had an uncanny ability to quickly and accurately read people; it didn't matter what the situation was, he was always within ninety-eight percent accuracy.

The welcoming smell of fried chicken passed through the screen door onto the front porch, Lucas looked out over the valley below. A warm feeling came over him, and a little disbelief of what his eyes were seeing. He turned back just in time to see his vision of the angel coming through the opening screen door.

"Well, Mr. Payne, you look as if most of the beast washed off of you and down the drain." Lucas was going to speak but he knew that he couldn't. He just stood there, looking stupid. He tried to clear his throat, but couldn't. Finally, he swallowed hard and nodded toward the angel that had spoken to him. My God, what a dumb ass he thought he must look like. She smiled at Lucas and turned to open the screen saying, "Pap-Paw, Mr. Payne, ya'll wash up now; dinner's almost ready."

The Ancient One put his hand on Lucas's shoulder as he turned to follow the angel. He leaned way over toward Lucas's head and said, "She has that affect on all young fellars there, Rider." He let out a chuckle as he opened the door.

Lucas just shook his head and followed her lead. He knew that the old man was absolutely right. Her beauty was beyond words, and that soft, soothing voice went right along with the rest of her. Lucas only knew too well because this was the second time that he had been totally dumbfounded by her.

As Lucas washed his hands he was busy looking over this great cabin, and he listened to the sounds from the kitchen. Once again the old familiar feeling came over him. It was like a built in self-defense system that always let him know when something heavy was about to come down. He turned and glanced to the left, then to the right. He caught a movement toward the screen door to his left, rear side.

Quickly he turned with a sharp, defensive move. Suddenly from out of nowhere, a firm hand came down upon his left shoulder. He pulled down quick and hard into the direction of the hand that had found him. He was looking directly into the face of the Ancient One. "Calm down, Rider, everything's okay here. Have a seat over there."

Lucas pulled out the heavy oak chair and sat down. He was looking at the perfectly fried chicken, a big bowl of mashed potatoes with a side of gravy, another bowl of fresh, southern style fried corn and a plate of hot, steaming biscuits being placed on the table. "This is great," Lucas said as the Ancient One passed the chicken to him.

They ate the meal in silence until they were finished. The old man asked, "Rider, would ya like some coffee?"

"Sure thing, that sounds about right," Lucas replied. The old man nodded toward Cyrista and she was instantly on her feet and moving toward the counter.

"We'll take it on the porch, child," the Ancient One said as he made his way toward the screen door.

Despite the grandeur of the view from the front porch, Lucas was feeling the hammer that was about to fall. "Rider," the Ancient One said, just as Cyrista gracefully moved through the screen door with three cups of coffee. "We need to talk. If you would be so kind to let me go first; I know that you'll have a lot of questions when I finish, but I'll be able to eliminate many of them by kickin' this here off."

Lucas was expecting this, and he was determined to be cool. He sat back in the old high-back rocking chair, one of many that lined the porch. He looked over at the Ancient One, nodded his head in understanding of what was said, and sipped the coffee, Cyrista had handed him. He looked over at Cyrista and gave her a slight smile.. The coffee was perfect: two sugars and a little cream. Now, how in the hell did she know how he took his coffee? This shit was getting a little spooky.

Who in the hell were these people? How were they able to read him so well? Lucas had been a closed book forever, spending most of his time alone. Hell, he had spent most of his whole life alone; he preferred it that way. Due to his lifestyle, he had always been a totally unpredictable person.

Even the cops that had been after him for so long told him that he was the most unpredictable son-of-a-bitch they had ever tried to nail. The bastards never could catch him with anything: no drugs, no money, so they finally hit him with a conspiracy charge. It held up well enough to cost him two years in the joint. Justice in the good old U.S. of A was a joke to Lucas.

He felt like the government had shit on him ever since he had turned of age to be shit on. He knew this from his younger days in the military. They went anywhere and killed anyone; it didn't matter. All was done for God and country. Some self-righteous bastards hiding behind the red tape of bureaucracy gave orders. He knew that he had been had, and it pissed him off, but he wrote that part of his life off as being young and dumb.

Lucas refocused on the Ancient One with greater intensity than before. "Rider, when you rode up here, it was not just chance that brought you to our door. We know where you had been, what you had done, what you have been through. You are either the luckiest son-of-a-bitch alive or you have the strongest instinct for survival of any man that I've had the pleasure of breaking bread with. I think it's the latter."

Lucas started to interrupt, but the Ancient One held up his left hand and stopped him.

The Ancient One continued, "You, Rider, and one other are the only to ever escape the bonds of those two evil bitches. How you came out from under their strong poison or drugs as you may refer to it, I'll never figure out. Not only did you shake off the drugs, but you also made some good moves, not to mention that you were able to ride here. There's a lot more, but I'll shut my mouth and let you fire away."

Lucas sat for a moment, looking first to Cyrista, then to the Ancient One, back and forth. He stood up, walked to the edge of the porch and stared down at the creek far below.

Against his better judgment, he turned toward Cyrista, looking directly into her ice-blue eyes, knowing his mistake but not caring. His mind was racing; his heart was pounding hard and his stomach dropped into an empty feeling despite the meal he had just eaten.

He knew what to do: Run. Turn and run like hell and don't look back. He couldn't move. All he could do was look deeper and deeper into those eyes.

His stomach came back and he began to breathe again. He didn't even realize that he had been holding his breathe. The spell between Cyrista and himself was broken. He turned to the old man who had moved while Lucas was in his trance. "Old man, I don't know how you know about me and what happened to me; all I know is that I've walked into something as crazy as hell and I'm in way over my head. I would like to thank you and Cyrista for a wonderful meal and for your kindness. I don't want to know anymore.

I've had a bad experience, not my first, but definitely the most bizarre. I've survived it and now it's time for me to load up my Harley and ride my ass out of these mountains."

"Rider," the Ancient One said, "That would be a wise thing to do, I understand. It'll be dark in less than an hour and these mountain roads are quite tricky, as you very well know. I think that you should stay over tonight and ride out in the morning when you're all fresh."

Lucas thought for a minute and agreed that would be the best thing to do. He turned toward the steep steps leading to the motel.

"Mr. Payne," Cyrista said softly, "I'll walk down with you. You'll need some clean sheets and towels. I know that you need them cause you were pretty scraped up when you rode in here…the night before last."

Lucas stopped dead in his tracks. He held onto Cyrista's last words: "when you rode in here the night before last." He smiled at her, nodded and said, "Only if you call me Lucas. Mr. Payne is much too formal for an old Harley rider like me."

Lucas's mind was once again racing. What the hell is going on here? The ride he had planned for the past two years seemed to have turned into an episode from the Twilight Zone.

He made the turn to the left to go to his room as Cyrista walked across the small lot into the storage room behind the office.

He went straight to the television and turned it on. It was one of the two stations he could pick up. The news was still on and the last weather report was giving the five-day forecast. Sure as hell, he had lost one complete day.

He felt the blood rushing into his head. He slowly sat down in the small, green armchair.

Cyrista walked through the open door carrying an arm full of sheets and towels. Watching her from where he sat he observed her very graceful movement. She was, no doubt, in one word grace. She made every move count; she was quick and efficient; nothing but total smoothness. He was so taken by her that it was making him crazy.

Going against his better judgment, he asked Cyrista to sit down and talk with him. Sitting on the edge of the bed, she crossed her long, shapely legs in front of her as she looked him directly in the eyes.

Taking a deep breath as he leaned forward in his chair placing his arms on his knees, Lucas began, "Cyrista, I need you to enlighten me on what is going in here."

"I've had quite a time for the past few days. Hell, I've even lost a day. This isn't easy for me to say, but it has to be said. I could make excuses for myself but that's just not my style. I allowed my little head to do my thinking for me and it has landed me in this dilemma. The only good thing to come out of it is meeting you and that great old man sitting up there on the side of the mountain. That is no "come on" line; it's just the truth.

"I set out on this ride to get my shit back together. It's my first ride in over two years. I might as well tell ya, I just got out of prison. For some reason I felt compelled to tell you that. Anyway, I came on this ride to relax and get my head together; so far it's been anything but that. I've been screwed, drugged, scratched, bruised, confused, streaked, and scared.

"I'm not very good at riddles or guessing games, they aggravate and annoy me to the point of pissing me off. You and the old man have been nothing but straight up with me." Lucas got to his feet. He looked at Cyrista, shook his head, and gently, in a very low voice said, "It's time for ya'll to come clean with me."

At that instant, the Ancient One came through the door. "What's the point in going through all that explaining, Rider? You said that you were riding on out of here in the morning."

Lucas didn't say a word. He only stared at the old man for a moment and then walked past him through the door. He walked to the end of the hall of the small motel. The small grassy area was well kept, just as everything else here. At the end of the grass was a well-beaten pathway. Listening to the stream running down the narrow gorge, he followed the path. Lucas didn't know where he was headed; he just needed room.

Walking slowly, he was overwhelmed with the feeling that he had been there before. When he stopped walking he was standing at the gate of a small cemetery. It included only six headstones; no doubt it was a family plot. He walked through the gate with his eyes focused on the largest headstone there. It was a double stone, one of those 'his' and 'hers' deals.

It was as if he was drawn to the stone as he walked toward it, he read the inscription he couldn't move his legs. They were like lead, as they had been in a bad dream that he used to have as a kid in which someone would be chasing him but he could barely run because his legs would barely move.

He tried to turn and move, but his legs wouldn't let him. Staring down at the stone he read the chiseled names in the marble: May they finally rest in peace. Cyrista and Lucas Payne.

Lucas wasn't sure how long he had been standing there when he shook off whatever had, had a hold on him. He felt very cold and the sun was far below the mountain, it was almost dark. Cyrista was standing next to him with her arm around his waist and her head on his shoulder.

Softly she spoke, "It's my mamma and papa. I miss them, Lucas. I was very young when it happened, but I can remember the happy times; the laughter and the love we all had. It was wonderful. Let's go, Lucas. You're freezing and you look as if you had seen a ghost."

Lucas regained the use of his legs, and everything else seemed to be working. He could feel the warmth coming from Cyrista's warm and close body. They turned and walked through the small gate when it hit him how cold he was. Cold? Hell! He was damn near frozen. Luke put his arm around Cyrista's shoulder and they pulled closer and closer as they walked toward his room.

They walked down the dimly lit hallway without saying a word to each other. When they reached his room the door was closed. Without letting go of Lucas, Cyrista pushed the door open.

Luke was still about half numb from whatever had a hold of him. The gentle, but passionate kiss that Cyrista gave him totally brought him back to his full senses. She had her body fully and firmly pressed against his body. Lucas responded, her passion increased. Her hands moved from the back of his neck to the middle of his back with smooth, easy rhythm. Standing there locked in the passionate embrace, Cyrista could not help but feel Lucas's excitement rising. His excitement rose, she pressed her body harder against his. They both broke the steamy lock of their lips at the same time.

Taking a deep breath and letting it out slowly, Cyrista moved her lips to the base of the left side of his neck. His head was tilted back to the right as he drew in a breath of air. At the moment he was about to talk, Cyrista said, "Don't talk, Lucas. Sometimes you just have to let things happen their own way. Trust me." Her soft-spoken words were warm on the side of his neck, but they felt warmer in his heart than anywhere else. Cyrista's grip around Lucas's neck tightened as she lowered herself onto the bed. Lucas bent over her slowly. He had put a hand on each side of her head on the bed as he looked down at this angel. It was hard for him to understand why this was happening. She unlocked her hands from the back of his neck and slid up in the bed, slipping off her sandals as she moved. Her bare legs were totally exposed to Lucas's view as her short cotton sundress rode up on her hips.

Lucas was standing straight up now, looking down at this beauty. It was more than he could stand; he'd lost all power of reasoning. He knew what would happen if he didn't stop this, but he was powerless. His eyes moved from her toes to where her short dress had moved. Her panties were exposed just below the dress and he saw that there was a little wet spot exactly where one should be.

Looking down and seeing this made him crazy. He lost any control that he may have had. The animal in him had taken over and he was ripping at his shirt and kicking off his boots at the same time.

Cyrista moved up to the top of the bed. She was sitting up, and with her usual graceful movement she pulled her little dress up over her head and dropped it to the floor. Now she sat with her arms extended behind her down to the bed holding her up. Her breasts were exposed. She had not been wearing a bra. Lucas gazed down at the silky smooth breasts and her lovely nipples. They looked like two rose buds in the spring that were about to bloom. This was, no doubt, perfection.

As he knelt down on the bed, Cyrista reached around with her right hand and slowly unbuttoned his jeans. Her fingers moved down to the zipper and slowly pulled it downward. As usual, Lucas wasn't wearing underwear. When the zipper reached its end, Lucas's excitement was standing full and straight. She let out a small gasp and in a hushed whisper said, "Oh, my."

Any uncertainty that either of them had was now gone. Lucas lowered his jeans to his knees and rolled over to his side to finish the execution of ridding himself of his last stitch. Cyrista rolled over on Lucas, straddling him. She slowly moved her wet panties up and down Lucas's long excitement.

It was on, they tasted each other's love and made love until exhaustion took them to frantic breathing and left them gasping for air. They lay there, holding each other until they both regained composure and then they made love again and again. It was not until total exhaustion took them into a deep sleep that they stopped.

Morning came and they woke at the same time. It was more like one person waking than two separate people. They were holding each other as if their lives depended upon it. Cyrista began to slowly kiss Lucas on the cheek and moved the kisses down to his neck. It took but a minute of this and they were locked in a passion as strong as it had been when they left off the night before.

Chapter Three

By the time that Lucas had finished with his shower and the rest of his grooming Cyrista was gone. What he did find was a pot of coffee, a cup, and plenty of cream and sugar.

He sat in his room and half-assed listened to the morning news and weather report. He sipped the coffee it slowly came to him what he would have to do. He knew for sure that he was in trouble. Every time in his past that he had felt good about someone it had landed him in trouble one way or another. He wasn't sure what to say or do about what he had been through in the past few days. Most of all, he hoped Cyrista felt the same about him as he did about her.

He left the bag and the rest of his gear in the room; he didn't even bother to close the door as he left the room. One thing that he loved about his old Harley was the way it always started right up. It might take only one or two turnovers and 'BAM', it was running.

Pulling out onto the road he looked toward the motel and saw Cyrista coming across the little bridge in the back of the motel. She looked as fresh and bright as she always did. Lucas went through the gears he was thinking of nothing but Cyrista. He hoped that she didn't think he was making a quick getaway. The thought had come to him, 'you bastard, run.' She would find out soon enough that he had not run out. She would find the door open and see his gear still in the room.

After he hit fifth gear, he saw a road sign that said, "Murphy - 5 miles". Then he saw a highway sign: 64. Holy shit, had he ever been turned around. He now knew exactly where he was. That, at least, made him feel better about things.

The last account that he'd had was when he was with the two witches. The thought of all that craziness sent a cold chill down his spine and his temper flashed. He would deal with that shit later.

He came to the crest of the mountain he could see the small town of Murphy. Lucas had always loved this part of the country; it was so clean and peaceful and warm. To the left of the city café was a phone booth. He would call Florida and tell his brother that he would be a few days later than he had planned. As a matter of fact, he would tell him not to expect him until he saw him pulling up. That should about cover it all.

He called the number but had to leave a message with the answering service. He walked down the sidewalk toward the Harley. He peeked inside the window of the café and saw that it was pretty busy. He walked over to the bike and got his smokes out of the front pouch. What the hell, he might as well go in and get some breakfast. Everyone in the place watched him as he had pulled up so why not give them a complete show. Lucas would be on his toes from this point on.

He opened the screen door to the café and walked inside. There were a few eyes on him. He knew how these small towns were because he had grown up in a similar town himself. Most of the people in the café were too busy eating and talking to one another to pay much attention to him.

He spotted an empty booth toward the back of the room and as he made his way to it an old timer looked up and said, "nice looking cycle you're ridin' there, boy."

Lucas thanked the old man for the compliment. The last thing he wanted to do was have a long conversation with an old man who called a Harley a 'cycle'.

"That there one o' them Harley Davidson's?" the old man asked long after Lucas had passed him by.

"Yes, sir, that's what it is all right," replied Lucas as he slid into the booth. Thank God that the waitress was quick and had moved in between Lucas and the old man. She winked and smiled as she put the silverware down on a clean napkin.

"Something to eat, Mister, or just coffee?"

"Both" said Lucas, looking directly at the waitress for the first time. She took his order and was back in a flash with "his coffee. "Damn," Lucas thought to himself. This is one fine looking little honey.

The waitress came with his order and as she set it on the table in front of him, she asked, "You're not from around these parts, are ya'?"

Lucas thought that she was either just making small talk or she was flirting with him in her simple country way. "No," Lucas replied with a slight smile. "I'm from Tennessee, the northwestern part, up on the Tennessee River: Kentucky Lake area. I'm just passing through."

"Don't look now," she said, "but there's a big ol' ugly fellar sitting down there a the end of the counter that asked me if I knew ya, and he's been checkin' ya out."

Lucas looked up at the little honey and said, "Well now, maybe he's just shy and he doesn't know how to tell me he loves me." This got a great big chuckle out of the quiet little waitress.

"More coffee, funny man?"

"Sure, why not?

"Say, what's your name?" asked Lucas as he set down the spoon.

"I'm Cissy," she replied, extending her right hand toward Lucas. He introduced himself as Lucas Payne as they shook hands.

"Well, Lucas Payne, it's good to meet ya. We don't get many new faces around here." Her voice then dropped low, "Watch your back, Lucas. I know the polecat that was askin' bout ya and he's no good. He really thinks he's something since he tied up with them." Then she turned and was gone instantly.

Lucas walked to the cash register to pay for his breakfast. Another waitress was there instead of Cissy. Damn, Lucas thought. He really wanted to ask her what she meant by "tied up with them". Just as quick as she disappeared she returned.

"I got this one, Becky. You're order is up." She winked at Lucas as he handed her the ticket and a twenty. "Here's your change, sir; thank you and come back and see me, ya here?"

She handed Lucas the change she held on to it slightly so that he would notice the piece of paper on top. He quickly folded it with the money and shoved it into his pocket.

He made his way out the door and to his Harley and could feel the eyes on his back all the way. After climbing onto the Harley, his eyes locked with those of the big, ugly man standing at the screen door. After a short but intense stare-down, Lucas started the bike and pulled out.

He rode slowly down the road thinking about what had just happened back at the restaurant. What in the hell did these people want with him? It was really beginning to piss him off. On the left he spotted a small Quick Mart. He pulled into the lot in front of the gas pumps. Not wasting any time, Lucas filled up the Harley and went inside to pay. As he reached into his pocket he remembered the note from Cissy. He held the note and the money low so that it was behind the counter, quickly peeling out a five and asked for a pack of smokes. As the girl behind the counter reached for his brand he put the note in his front shirt pocket. Lucas walked out to the Harley he opened the note and read it. It was short and simple: "Meet me here at 6:00…Cissy". Below was a little map to the spot.

Riding back to the motel his thoughts were of Cyrista. This whole thing was crazy, but Lucas was having fun with it and Cyrista seem to make it all worthwhile.

No one was around when Lucas got back to his room. He was glad for that. When he opened the door he saw that the room had been cleaned and all of his gear was placed neatly in the corner next to the T.V. Cyrista had left a note on the bed. Lucas picked it up and read it.

"My dearest Lucas, I'll see you at lunch…Love, Cyrista".

One of those ear-to-ear smiles came across Lucas's face. "Love, Cyrista," he said out loud as he lowered himself to the bed. He could still smell her sweet scent as he drifted off into a two-hour nap.

It was half past noon when Cyrista came down to Lucas's room. He was out by his Harley, wiping it down when she came around the corner. Her hair was in a braid and she wore sunglasses with a tight fitting pair of jeans and boots. Man, oh man, did she look good.

Lucas stepped toward her to greet her and before he knew it her arms were around his neck and her lips were pressed tightly against his. "It's good to see you too," Lucas said as she loosened her grip.

"What have you been up to, Lucas Payne?" before he could answer she said, "I'm starving, let's ride."

They rode through Murphy and beyond until Cyrista pointed to a place up on the right. All the time she had sat back and enjoyed the ride. Lucas could tell it wasn't her first time to ride on the back of a bike. He hardly knew she was back there except for the occasional rub on his back.

The little café was sitting back off of the road in a clearing with the back of it against the wall of a mountain. Most everything along these mountain roads was built this way. They dismounted and were walking up the steps when the smell of fish frying hit him. "Smells good," Lucas said, turning toward Cyrista.

"Yeah," she said with a warm smile. "I hope you like fish, it's the best in these parts."

"Well, well…Howdy!" Cyrista shouted to an old woman. She looked to be as old as the Ancient One, Lucas thought.

"Howdy, Granny Franks. How ya been feelin'?" Cyrista asked the old woman with a tone of concern.

"Oh, ya know, darlin', not too awful bad for an

old woman. I can still sit up and take nourishment." Cyrista laughed at the old woman's humor. "You two love-birds sit where ya want to and I'll be right there."

"Now, Granny, how do you know if we're love-birds or not?" Cyrista asked in a playful manner.

"Child, I've been a knowin' ya since you were hatched and I can see it in yer eyes and the way yer holdin' onto that good-lookin' fellar. And if'n his ears git any redder they'll bleed!" Then the old woman let out a big, hearty chuckle.

Holding tight to Lucas's hand, Cyrista led him to a small patio in the very rear. There was room for five tables on it and she led him to one by the railing. The side of the mountain was no more than twenty feet away and there was a small stream running against the bottom of it.

"All right, this is beautiful. What a great place," said Lucas as he looked all around.

"Glad ya like it. I thought you would. It's my favorite place to come and eat and relax and Granny cooks the best trout in the whole world. She makes her own batter and she won't share the recipe with no one. She says she'll leave the recipe to me when she's gone; says its too good not to be passed on."

Granny came out onto the patio carrying a pitcher and two glasses. She set them on the table while stealing a glance at Lucas.

"Granny, this here is Lucas Payne. The old woman staggered back a few steps as if she had been shot.

Then she turned white as a ghost. "Granny…Granny, are you okay?" Cyrista asked as she got to her feet and helped poor old Granny sit down.

"Holy smokes, child! What ya tryin' to do to poor old Granny? I was lookin' at him and a thinking how much he looked like Lucas, then ya go an try to put me in the ground by sayin' that's who it is."

"But, Granny, that's his name. He rode in here a few days ago; oh, that's another story." Cyrista was trying to hold back a smile but it kept leaking through.

Granny jumped to her feet like a youngster, "Holy smokes, now ya got me burnin' y'alls lunch." She was gone to the kitchen with a quick hobble.

When Granny was out of earshot, both Cyrista and Lucas broke down in a roar. They laughed until tears were streaming down their cheeks. Lucas lit up a cigarette and drank some of the sweet tea that Granny had brought out. Cyrista looked over to Lucas and said, "Poor old Granny. I feel terrible, but that was too much."

Lucas was still halfway laughing as he wiped the tears from his eyes. He was looking around at the grounds that the little café was built on. Little streams of sunlight made their way through the trees and sparkled off the small drops of water that leaked from the side of the mountain. The moss and ferns that grew on its smooth rocks looked like an emerald green blanket and the little wild flowers were a decorative pattern. Things like this could touch an emotion in Lucas that was seldom reached. He sat in a state of total tranquility; it felt good to him. He had always called such feelings 'God's little rewards'.

Granny came from the kitchen with two platters. One was piled high with golden brown filets of fish and the other with fries and hush puppies. The old woman was smiling as she set the platters down in front of Cyrista and Lucas. "I'll be back with y'alls beans in just a zip." She gave Lucas a big smile and a wink then moved out with a hobble more slowly than before. Lucas figured that she was trying to conserve fuel.

"Granny knew my daddy, Lucas. Matter of fact, she practically raised him; so you can imagine why it was such a shock for her when I told her who you were. I suppose I should have been a little more considerate of how and when I told her."

Granny came back through the doors leading to the patio carrying two bowls; one was filled with a colorful vinegar slaw. "I'll talk to y'all before ya leave; some more folks have come in."

"Granny, where is Lily?" asked Cyrista.

"Oh, she's a runnin' late. You know how she is when she gits a new man." Granny let out a chuckle as she turned and left the patio.

Lucas looked over at Cyrista and saw that she too was having a good little chuckle. "Is this some kind of private joke?" he asked.

"No," said Cyrista, still chuckling. "You'd have to know Lily. She's Granny's twin sister, but they are as different as night and day. Lily is so funny, Lucas. You'll see what I mean when she gets here."

Lucas began to fill his plate from the platters and bowls that Granny had left them. After tasting a little bit of everything he asked Cyrista if Granny would consider adopting him.

She smiled at Lucas and said to him, "Don't give it another thought, Lucas; she already has."

"Cyrista, we didn't order this."

"Ha ha," Cyrista laughed. "Granny knows what to bring me when I come in here. It's a tradition with us."

They both ate until they couldn't stand any more. Lucas was thinking the whole while that he'd never eaten trout that tasted like this. He really wasn't that fond of trout until today. When they finished there was still enough for two or three people to eat: if only they were big eaters.

"Don't worry, Lucas, nothing will go to waste. Granny will pack it up for us. She always puts out this much. She wants to make sure there is enough for me to take home to Pap-Paw. I like it because I won't have to cook tonight. Pap-Paw will feast on this all night; and if he says it once, he'll say it twenty times: 'that woman sure has a way with trout.'" Cyrista had dropped her voice to imitate how Pap-Paw would sound and the results left both of them laughing. Lucas was seeing another side of Cyrista and he liked it. So far, there was nothing about her that he did not like.

Granny came back with a pot of coffee and two cups. After she poured the coffee she looked Lucas directly in the eyes and said, "If'n I didn't know any better, I'd swear you were my Lucas. Now ya sit here lookin' like him an carryin' the same name. Now, I ain't one to get spooked 'bout nuthin', but this here's a little spooky." You two sittin' here like this turns back the hands of time. The both ya come ridin' up on that big ol' motorcycle. If that don't beat all; takes me back thirty years."

Granny began to clear the table. She was mumbling something under her breath when Cyrista got up and began to help her. All of a sudden Granny snipped, "Hey! I can handle this, here; I can still do my job. Sit your little ass down there and enjoy ya self. I'll take this in yonder and pack it up for that ornery old Pap-Paw of ya's."

"Yes, ma'am," Cyrista replied politely.

"Granny and Pap-Paw go way back. They adore each other. It's a real hoot when they get together; you can see their eyes light up.

"The story goes that they were lovers when they were younger. I never knew my own granny; she died before I was born. Granny Franks has been the only granny I've ever known. Her and Pap-Paw raised me after mama and daddy were gone. Oh, Lucas, I love her so much."

Lucas reached over the table and held her little hand between his. She gave him a little smile as she wiped at a tear with her other hand. Cyrista then brought that hand down on top of Lucas's and, out of nowhere said, "Ya just have to let things happen sometimes. Lucas, it scares the hell out of me, but I can't help myself: I love you, Lucas Payne."

Lucas didn't move, but inside he felt as though he had been hit by lightning. Before he could even think the words flowed out from his mouth, "I love you too, Cyrista Payne." Through the shock of it all they could do nothing but sit there and look into each other's eyes.

Lucas had started it off; he had been quiet for most of the afternoon, now it was his turn. "Cyrista, what we've done and what we just said to each other can never be erased. It is set in our lives for as long as we each should live and longer; as long as people remember us."

"I couldn't have said it better, Lucas." She sat there still holding onto his hand as if her life depended on it.

"There is nothing I would rather do than sit here all afternoon and talk about you and me, which we'll do real soon. But at this time, I think we need to talk about what's going on up here and the part that I play in it all. I've got a pretty good idea, but there's also a lot that I don't know and I need you to fill in the spaces for me. I can't go into this half-assed and expect to come out on top."

Cyrista's look changed. She let go of Lucas' hand and poured them some more coffee. "You're right, Lucas. Your timing couldn't be worse. You jumped and have landed in the middle of a hornet's nest. This is the beginning of their holiday time and it will last for two months."

"They, Cyrista? Who in the hell are they? All I know about 'they' is how I got tied up with them when I first came here." Lucas was trying not to sound so aggravated as he spoke but it came through anyway.

"I've got to hand it to you, Lucas Payne. When we speak of 'they', you went to the top of the list. 'They', Lucas, are who we are talking about." A note of aggravation was in Cyrista's voice as she lashed back at Lucas.

"It is those two that lead this evil group of people, or whatever they are."

"Let me start from the beginning, the way Pap-Paw told it to me a long time ago. He came up here with his family to get away from the fast growing and moving population of the cities. His papa was a simple man and he wanted to raise his family in the clean, pure and simple ways of God and life. They loaded up the wagon with what little they had and headed southwest. Pap-Paw was very young, but he says that he remembers what an adventure it was.

"They had been traveling for about two weeks, on what now would be called I-95, when his papa turned off the main road. The going was rough for about ten days. This was still pretty wild country back then. One day they stopped early to eat. Pap-Paw knew that something was up when his papa sent the two oldest boys for firewood. After they ate the rabbits and squirrels they had shot or trapped the day before, his papa ordered the wagon to be unloaded; he thought the good Lord has led them to their utopia."

This was beginning to sound like the Westward movement story, but Lucas liked it. It was rich with Cyrista's family background, and anything that related to her Lucas wanted to know about. He thought of himself as a good storyteller, so he naturally loved hearing a good story.

"They built right on that very spot where they had had lunch that day. No one lives there anymore, but the cabin is still standing. I won't bore ya with the details of mountain survival back in those days, but the family did good. "Pap-Paw says that somehow his papa bought the land along the road. They built a travelers rest right on top of the very spot where the motel stands today.

"More and more people came to the area; most of them for the same reason that the Payne family did. They put up a meeting house that served the people for just about every activity that they had; any celebration, dances, church, court, everything. Pap-Paw says that his papa became a self-proclaimed preacher.

"There is an end to this Lucas, I promise." Cyrista

said in a laughing manner. "Anyway, Pap-Paw's two older brothers couldn't stand all of their papa's self righteousness so they moved back up to the cabin where the family had lived.

"Times were changing and the two brothers had also changed. More and more auto travel became accessible to the area and the brothers went out to the nearest big towns to get jobs. They were gone for about two years, when one day they both showed up driving a nice car.

"They moved back into the cabin and were rarely seen anywhere. The story goes that they became the biggest moon shiners in the state of North Carolina, and the southeastern section of Tennessee. I've heard some of the old timers say that they had a natural talent for brewing the best shine that was ever made."

Lucas was really enjoying the story now. It was good to know that Cyrista had outlaws on her side of the family. He sat back and sipped on the cold beer that Granny had brought him.

Cyrista continued on with the story. "This practice went on for years. Their papa and mama had passed away, but Pap-Paw said that his brothers had kept close ties with them to the end. The brothers never forgot where they had come from; they came by often leaving money for their parents. Pap-Paw says that he became very close to his brothers in spite of the big age difference. He would go up to the cabin with his brothers and stay for weeks at a time. That's another story; I'll tell that one to ya another at time. We'll be here all night if I go into all of that." They both laughed and Cyrista went on.

"Pap-Paw and his older sister took over the traveler's rest that had since turned into a more modern motel. Times were good; the area was growing, tourist trade had developed, and more and more good people came to settle in the area. People with dreams and a little money opened businesses; and before long, Murphy became a thriving little community.

The brothers had gotten married and now had families of their own, but they kept the operation up at the cabin going and growing. It was said that they could both retire with enough money that their children would never have to do work.

"One day one of the brothers drivers came down to the motel and told Pap-Paw that he had better get up to the cabin, that there had been big trouble. When Pap-Paw got up there it looked like a war zone. The brothers had a customer out of New York that wanted to take over their operation, but the brothers saw things different.

"All of the out buildings were burned to the ground, the barn was blown to hell, and there was a hole in the earth about six feet deep. That was where the still used to sit. Pap-Paw said the ugly part was the bodies lying all over the place. There were six of them in all; one of them was his oldest brother.

"They brought him down the mountain and buried

him next to his mama and papa in our little family cemetery out back that you found the other day. Pap-Paw and the surviving brother went back up on the mountain to clean up the rest of the mess. When they got there the other five bodies were gone, along with the two cars that the thugs had driven up there. The cars had been shot and blown to hell so they knew that they had not been driven off. There wasn't a trace of anything; it would have been quite a chore cleaning it all up. The brothers had used a lot of dynamite during the battle, so everything was scattered far and wide. They never found anything.

"Pap-Paw said that was the beginning of the dark times to fall on our valley. It was about ten days later when his brother came by the motel. He had his wife, two sons, and everything that they could get in that old car. His brother told Pap-Paw that it was time to move on and that he should do the same; he said that he was going to the coast. He had always dreamed of living by the sea, and he loved to fish anyway.

"It was about two years later when Pap-Paw got a letter and a few pictures from his brother. They had ended up in Nag's Head, North Carolina. One of the pictures was of his brother and two boys standing on a big fishing boat. On the back of the boat in bold writing is said PAYNE and SONS - Nag's Head, NC. His brother had started fishing and couldn't stop. The last word we had from his sons was they had about thirty boats in their fishing fleet.

"The widow of his oldest brother took her kids and moved into town. She bought the biggest house that she could find. It never seemed to satisfy her so she built on three additions to it before she was happy. She was a shrewd ole gal when it came to investing her money.

"Her and the kids lived there like royalty; they had maids, butlers, and even had a driver for the big ole car that they had. She became quite the social butterfly of Murphy. The kids went off to the best schools that money could buy; they never came back to her to live. The last word that we had was that they both were living in New York City."

"You have got a very rich family history Cyrista, but what has this got to do with what's going on here now?" Lucas took a drink off of his third beer and lit up another cigarette.

"Patience my dear. I couldn't tell you the second part without telling you the first part or you might be totally confused." Cyrista told him. She flashed her eyes and smiled at him. That was all that it would take to melt Lucas down and she knew it.

"Like I told you, Pap-Paw was the youngest of the Payne children. His sister was the closest in age to Pap-Paw and she was fifteen years older than he was. She fell in love with a salesman that traveled and use to stay at the motel when he came up this way. He sold farming tools and supplies. He was a good man, a simple man; they married and she moved up to Asheville with him. They had a good life together, and it was partially due to Pap-Paw.

"After she had moved, Pap-Paw was going through things. The storeroom was packed and Pap-Paw needed the room. He found a big old tin way back on the shelf in the back of the storage room. When he opened it, it was full of old money. The only thing that he could figure out was that it was the money that the two brothers use to give to his mama and papa.

"Pap-Paw was young and inexperienced, but he was smart enough to realize it. He took the money up to the big house that his sister-in-law was living in. He told her the story about finding it and where he believed that it came from. Like I said earlier, she was a good woman and a smart one too, when it came to money matters. She took the money and invested it for Pap-Paw. The returns started coming in and Pap-Paw split every penny of it with his sister; they had made a lot of money. Then one day they split off their partnership and each went their own way with investing.

"Life was good for Pap-Paw; he was the youngest businessman in the area. He had everything he wanted; he had money, nice clothes, a new car, and plenty of good looks. My Lord Lucas, he was a good-looking man. He was having fun and enjoying life, but he was lonely. He missed the closeness that he had with his family. He was the only one left in the valley except for his ole sister-in-law, and she was gone most of the time. She was either in New York with her kids or off somewhere in Europe.

"He belonged to the local merchants association; they met once a month and Pap-Paw had become good friends with a few of the members. After a meeting one night, he was invited to dinner by ole Mr. O'Dull. He liked Pap-Paw and he wanted him to court his daughter. Pap-Paw said it was love at first sight for both of them.

"Everything was great. They saw each other at every chance they had. Pap-Paw ate more meals at the O'Dull's than he did at home. They made plans to be married; that was when Pap-Paw began building the cabin behind the motel. As soon as it was finished they would be married.

"The big day finally came. Pap-Paw said it was a grand affair, he said that she was the most beautiful bride that could have ever been. Life was good for Pap-Paw and my granny Mary. He had never been happier in his entire life. They had been married for a little over three years when my daddy was born.

"About two years later, Pap-Paw heard that someone had bought the land where the old homestead had been. His papa had never filed a claim on the land and the brothers thought that it would not be a very good idea due to the nature of their business.

"Pap-Paw and Granny Mary planned a picnic up

by the ole cabin. Pap-Paw wanted Mary to see it before the new owners moved up there. He didn't know what their plans were; maybe they would tear it down or burn the ole cabin.

"They loaded up the car and the three of them were off to the ole homestead for a fun filled afternoon. They drove as far as they could, but the ole road had grown over so they had to hike the last quarter mile or so."

"They unloaded the basket of goodies and a blanket to sit on. Pap-Paw says that it was a perfect spring day for a picnic. Mary loved the old cabin and the spot where it was built. She loved the stories Pap-Paw told of living there and spending time with his big brothers after they had taken it over.

"Pap-Paw said that he saw something a little strange on the walk to the cabin after they had left the car. He says that he saw a woman on a big black horse off in the distance; the strange thing about her was how she was dressed. She was wearing what looked to be a long black robe. Pap-Paw had never seen anyone dress that peculiar before, and especially riding a horse. Granny Mary didn't see her and Pap-Paw didn't want to spook her by saying anything or pointing her out to her.

"My papa had gone to sleep on the blanket under a big shade tree. Mary told Pap-Paw that she wanted to stretch her legs and find a place to pee. There used to be an outhouse but it was lost in the big battle when his brothers were up there. She kissed him and said that she would be back in a little bit. That was the last time that Pap-Paw ever saw her; she just vanished.

"Mary didn't come back and Pap-Paw started to worry. He called to her, but he didn't get an answer. He picked up my daddy and they began a search for her. Pap-Paw ran back to the car with daddy in and sped to town. He went straight to the O'Dull's house. Quickly he told what happened. He left daddy with Mrs. O'Dull and told Mr. O'Dull to organize a search party.

"For the next ten days there was up to a hundred people in the search party. They had the best dogs brought in from the surrounding counties; but nothing, not even a trace.

"When Pap-Paw was totally exhausted, it took Mr. O'Dull and four other men to drag him off that mountain; they said he went crazy.

"When Pap-Paw regained his strength, he made arrangements for daddy to be looked after and the motel to be taken care of. For the next three years he looked for his lost love. People were really beginning to talk about him. Everyone thought that he was gone; that he had lost his mind to grief. Several of the newspapers wrote stories about him.

"He had let his beard grow long and scraggy and his hair was down to the middle of his back, he looked like a wild man. One morning when he was getting ready to head up the mountain, he went over to the O'Dull's to see daddy. The O'Dull's had taken up the raising of daddy.

"Pap-Paw reached over and caught a hold of daddy's hand to pick him up and give him a hug good-bye. Daddy kicked and screamed and cried until Pap-Paw put him down. Pap-Paw looked down at him and walked out. Pap-Paw returned that afternoon; he had shaved his beard and cut his hair and he looked human again.

"He stayed for dinner and they all talked openly about Mary being gone. When it was time to go, he looked over at daddy and asked him if he wanted to go home with him. Daddy stood up like a little man and told Pap-Paw that it was about time that he went home.

"Ever since that day they were inseparable. They did everything together; they worked together, hunted and fished, went to town together, everything. As daddy grew, they became more like brothers than father and son, and looked like it too.

"Life was good for both of them. Then the war came and daddy joined up; it broke Pap-Paws heart, but he understood. After all, he had raised him to be bold and daring. Daddy volunteered for the paratroopers and was assigned to the 82nd Airborne."

Lucas had a great big smile on his face so Cyrista stopped her story and asked him what he was smiling so big for. He told her that the 82nd was whom he served with when he was in the military. She told him that it didn't surprise her.

Cyrista went on with the story. "It was the 17th anniversary of Mary's disappearance and Pap-Paw went up on the mountain. He was lonely with daddy being gone and all. He took a picnic lunch and a blanket just like that dreadful day when Mary had vanished."

"After driving as far as he could, he left the car and started to hike the rest of the way up the mountain; he had basket and blanket in hand. Sitting there alone, his thoughts went from his beloved Mary to daddy. He ate his lunch and lay back on the blanket. It wasn't long until he drifted off into a dream filled sleep."

"When Pap-Paw woke up the sun was going down. He didn't worry about that because he knew every inch of that mountain like the kitchen in his own cabin. He gathered up his basket and blanket and started toward the car."

"By the time he got to where he had left the car it had gotten dark. The only problem was that the car was not where he had left it. It was gone; it took a lot to upset Pap-Paw. He figured someone, probably some boys, had stumbled upon it and took it out for a joy ride."

"Just as he was about to hike his way home, he heard something. Out of nowhere came a woman riding a big black horse and wearing a long black hooded robe. His thoughts raced back to the day Mary had vanished. He had seen such a woman earlier that day, riding a black horse and dressed in the same fashion."

"She rode up close to Pap-Paw and dropped her hood. She was one of the most beautiful women that he had ever seen. Her hair was long, thick and full of curls. The only thing that struck him as a little odd was that to the left of center was a small gray streak of hair several inches long."

"She looked him directly in his eyes and asked if he had lost something. He didn't answer. She went on to tell him that if he would follow her that he could find what he had lost. He walked behind her, she spoke again. "You have lost a lot up on this ole mountain over the years. I think that you would know better than to keep coming up here."

"They went on past the ole homestead, up to the crest and about half way down the other side of the mountain; up ahead he could see a fire burning. At that time the woman on the horse turned and said, 'I've got a surprise for you. Don't you like surprises?'"

"As they grew nearer to the fire he could see a cabin in the background. He had been all over this mountain and the cabin had not been there before. Three people were standing around the fire with their backs to him. The woman on horseback went around to the other side of the fire and addressed him. 'I told you that I had a surprise for you, and I do. Your auto isn't here.' She let out a loud evil laugh and tilted her head back and her finger pointed straight to his face. 'But I do have someone here to see you,' at that time the person standing closest to him turned to face him and dropped her hood."

"His heart dropped; he had no breath and he could not swallow. It took but a second for the sound of his heart to be the only sound that could be heard. He tried to move but couldn't. Words were forming and coming out of her mouth; but all he could hear was his blood rushing and the unsteady pounding in his temples."

"The unbelievable was happening. Mary was there, standing not three feet from him. She smiled and moved toward him, but he still couldn't move. She reached out and took him by the hand; his legs were weak and his breathing was fast. He tried to speak but nothing came out. Her arms were around him and she pulled her body close to his."

"Together they walked to a log close by the fire. He could now hear her sweet voice, 'It's all right my love, I'm here.' 'Mary, what are you doing here, where've you been all of this time?' she gave him a long passionate kiss and said, 'Not now my darling, you will understand every thing in just a short while.'"

Cyrista stopped; she looked at Lucas with a sad but loving look in her eyes. "Need I go on with the rest of this story?"

Lucas took a drink from the beer that he was

holding, then said, "This is one hell of a story Cyrista, but I think that I've got it figured out. Let me see how close I am to the right answers."

"No doubt the woman on the horse is a witch and the rest of the group around the fire are also. They drugged Pap-Paw and seduced him with the intent of making him a sacrifice for the ritual. There was never any Mary there; it was one of their evil tricks that they play to lure in their victims. How am I doin' so far?" She nodded at him and he went on.

"They prey on the weak and take control of their lives and their souls. The only time that they mess with anyone that is strong is for revenge. I do have one question, why were they after Pap-Paw, and even more so, why where they after me?"

She took the beer out of his hand, turned it up and killed it. "That's a good question Lucas. Remember my Pap-Paw's brothers, the moon shiners?" Lucas smiled and nodded to her and she went on. "They had no idea what or who the people from the east were. They were good customers, and they had money. Little did the brothers know that they were an evil coven trying to relocate down here."

"During the battle that took place on the mountain, the brothers killed five of their people; the five that were killed where the breeders for the coven. They had grossly under estimated the brothers. They thought it would be easy to take over everything. By doing this it set the coven back a hundred years or more. None of this was known until Pap-Paw was taken on the anniversary date of Mary's disappearance. He had never put it together, but it was the date of the brothers' battle."

"Since then, they have reorganized. They now make up in numbers what they had in strength. It is always a practice for them to seduce their strong victims in hopes to reproduce strong offspring."

"They took you by mistake." Lucas looked at Cyrista like he couldn't believe she would insult him.

"Gee, thanks a lot Cyrista."

"No, No," she said. "I didn't mean it that way. They had gotten bogus information on you; they thought you were part of this Payne clan. If you are it is so distant that it would go back at least four generations; which would make us all removed. Now, does that make you feel better all the way around?"

He laughed and got to his feet. "We had better get going Cyrista, your Pap-Paw is probably starving by now."

"Wait Lucas, don't you want to hear about how they got my daddy and Mama? And the letter?"

"Yes I do Cyrista, but it is time to move. You can tell me when we get back to the room."

They said their good-byes to Granny Franks and Lucas paid the bill and gave her a hug good-bye. They loaded up the food that Granny had carefully wrapped up and they were off.

Chapter Four

Lucas was thinking of the story that Cyrista had told him when he hit fourth gear. He and Cyrista saw it at the same time; there was an old hay wagon rolling out in front of them from a small road off to the right. Lucas yelled to Cyrista to hold on; he hit the brake hard and turned the front wheel to the right. They were going down, but they had missed the wagon. Lucas let off the brake and turned to the left; the front wheel was in the gravel but the bike was coming back up. At that instant he gunned the bike for all it was worth. They flew off the small culvert from the small side road and landed in the ditch with force. Lucas held hard and managed to bring the heavy ass Harley back up onto the road, without going down.

Lucas let out a big yell, "YEE-HA" as they slowed to a stop. A pickup truck coming from the opposite direction had not been so lucky; he had hit the wagon and overturned it.

Cyrista hit Lucas on his right shoulder and said, "Let's go baby, the cops will be here shortly." Lucas knew that she was right, but he also knew that the wagon rolling out into the road was no accident.

They made it back to the motel without any more incidents. Cyrista climbed off the Harley while Lucas held it. When he had the kick stand down, she threw her arms around his neck and gave him a big wet kiss. "That was some good riding back there, ole boy," she said with laughter in her tone.

"Hell," Lucas said, "if you're going to act like that we'll go back and do it again. All kidding aside Cyrista, someone set us up."

"I know," she said, "I've got to run up and feed Pap-Paw and take care of a few chores. Why don't you relax until I get back?"

He unloaded the food they had brought back, but not without pulling out a few pieces of fish for himself. He handed the rest to Cyrista and told her to try not to be too long; he had something to tell her when she got back. She smiled at Lucas and was gone. "Damn," he said aloud while shaking his head; "she's one cool customer. Most chicks would have come unplugged."

He unlocked the door to the room and went inside. Leaving the door open, he sat down on the bed and started munching on the fish. He thought about the afternoon that he had spent with Cyrista. He couldn't help but think of what an eventful and informative time that it had been; not to mention she said that she loved him. Yea!

"Cyrista, is that you darling?" the old man asked as she opened the screen door. He might be old but there was nothing wrong with his hearing; he could hear a mouse fart in a windstorm.

"Yes Pap-Paw". He's everything that you said he would be. He's a little rough around the edges, but he has a good heart. You have always said to measure a man by his heart, not by his looks or the weight of his wallet. I got an extra with him; I think he is good looking as well"

"We'll see how measures up child; if he hangs in here with us for the next few days and pays attention, he might just make it."

Lucas was sitting outside of the room on the curb of the sidewalk. His thoughts were of the story that Cyrista had told him, especially the parts of her Pap-Paw. That old man had really been through a lot of heartbreak in his lifetime. Lucas heard a little noise behind him. He turned to see the Ancient One standing there. "Damn Lucas said in a surprised tone. "Where did you come from? I didn't hear ya till you were right there."

The Ancient One chuckled a little and said, "It's an old Indian trick. Ha-ha! Your mind is preoccupied there, Rider. I'm sure that you have a lot to think about; it's not that often a man meets a woman like my Cyrista."

"You said a mouthful there my friend, but I was really thinking of you at the time, and then there ya are." Lucas tilted his head back and to the right to look up at the old man.

"Hey, Rider, take a little walk with me if ya would please."

"Sure," Lucas said as he staggered to his feet. "But I want ya to know that you're interrupting my busy schedule." They both laughed a little and the old man put his hand on Lucas' shoulder as they started to the end of the motel.

Lucas liked this old man; there was a connection between the two of them. It was more than Cyrista; it was like they were soul mates or something like that.

They walked to the end of the motel and down the path toward the little family cemetery. When they got to the gate, the old man swung it open. Over to the right was a bench made of big boulders that were used for the legs and a slab sitting on top of them to serve as the seat.

Lucas was looking at the headstones as the Ancient One took a seat on the bench. The last time that he had wondered out here and found the little cemetery his eyes had been stopped when they came up on the marker that bore his name. He looked to the right of that headstone now and saw that the name on it was Mary Payne. It read under the name…"Her Soul Came Home and to the Lord".

"I put that up after my night up on the mountain with those evil souls that took her from me." Lucas looked over to the Ancient One and saw a little fire coming from those old eyes.

"Cyrista told me of your ordeal that you had that

night, but she never said how you got out from up there."

The old man didn't hesitate; he went right into the story. "Rider, I was a lot younger and I was as strong as a stud horse back in those days. They did me like they did you. They gave me a strong drug that was supposed to render me helpless while they practiced their evil deeds."

"I came to before they could get to do whatever that they do to their victims, but they caught me and they dragged me outside by the fire. All that I could think of was my Mary. Every time that I would call her name they would laugh in a loud and hideous manner; then they would kick and spit on me as I lay there. Finally, the one that had been riding the black horse grabbed me by my hair and pulled my head up and said, 'Here is your precious Mary.' A woman wearing one of those black robes stepped up and pulled down her hood."

"It was Mary alright, in looks anyway. I reached up for her; she grabbed my hand and pulled me up to my knees. Then she spit in my face and called me a stupid man and laughed. She said 'If your mean, evil brothers had not started this, nothing would have ever happened to your precious Mary.'"

"The one that had been riding the horse yelled at her, 'shut up you fool' and slapped her across her face. Right then and there in front of my very eyes my Mary turned into a twin of the other one. They were busy laughing in their loud and hideous way to pay much mind to me. I don't know how I did what I did, but it happened."

"I jumped to my feet, Rider. I was in a rage; half crazed. I grabbed her up and pulled her up over my head. I told the rest of them to get back, but they wouldn't listen. They were too busy laughing and making sounds that I ain't ever heard a human make. They kept a comin' at me, spittin' and hissin' and talking some language I ain't never heard before."

"I let out a big roaring sound and charged at them. This got their attention and then I let her fly. When that bitch hit the fire it was all over. Those bitches and sons-of bitches scattered like flies. I saw my chance to get away and moved. I didn't get four or five feet from the fire when it happened. The one that I threw in the fire exploded. Hell, Rider, I ain't never seen such a thing. It was crazy."

Lucas stood there for a minute looking at the headstone of Mary Payne. He turned to the Ancient One, not knowing what to say. The words just came out: "Holy shit…exploded?"

They were staring at each other. "Yeah, just exploded." At the same time they were both roaring with laughter; you could hear them for miles.

"I'm sorry. I guess I haven't heard of anyone exploding before." Lucas was still laughing, "I'll bet that scared the hell out of you."

"It's okay, Rider. I ain't never thought of it that

way before. Hell, besides you, the only one that I've told it to was Cyrista. Looking back now, if you had told me such a wild story I might have had the same reaction." The Ancient One had a chuckle under his breath. "Yeah, it sure as hell did surprise me.

"Rider, that's my boy there next to where Mary would be. You remind me of him an awful lot. You even look somewhat like him. He was bigger than what you are. That's his lovely wife next to him, Cyrista's mama. I can be sure that he didn't have to go through the suffering of the heartbreak of missing her. I can thank the Lord for that anyway. They went together and it was quick too."

Lucas knew that the Ancient One was going to tell him what happened to them, so he didn't bother to ask.

"Ya know, Rider," the old man addressed Lucas in a low tone, "I've lived a long time; maybe to damn long, and I've seen all kinds of things happen. I've experienced pain, and lots of it. But I've never gone out and hurt anybody on purpose. Nor have I started anything with anyone.

"Those monsters claimed that my brother started this shit. I'll be the first to admit that they were no angels. Hell fire, they were good ol' country boys making shine. They sure as hell weren't the only ones doing it; they were just the unfortunate ones to get tied up with that evil bunch.

"I went up there and I saw what was done. All my

brother's did was try to protect what was theirs."

Lucas could see that the Ancient One was getting wound up. He still had a lot of fight left in him.

"I sure as hell didn't start this fight, but by God, Rider, I swear I'll finish it."

The old man went on, "My boy fought in the war, he wasn't scared of anything. When it was over and he came home I sat him down and told him all of what happened to me while he was gone. I wanted him to be prepared for anything that they might do or try to do to him. He wanted to get them as bad as I did.

"Rider, me and my boy were close. I mean we were best of friends. We did everything together. We were riders once upon a time; we loved it. Even after he and Cyrista were killed I still rode. We had a pair of Indian Chiefs that we ordered and picked up from the factory. It's a shame about them going out of business. They made a hell of a bike." Lucas smiled in agreement.

"Anyway, that evil bunch knew that they couldn't get my boy the way that they got you and me. He had made a friend during the war. His friend wasn't just anyone; he was the son of a gypsy king. I don't know what you know about them gypsies, but they know all about spells, potions, witches, and all that sort of stuff. He was on his way here when my boy got killed.

"I may as well get to the point. We were all riding one day. We were on our way home; I was out in the lead. We were coming around a corner and out of the middle of nowhere a big old hay wagon rolls out in front of us. I was lucky and managed to get around the back of it, but my boy and Cyrista weren't so lucky. A pickup truck was coming the other way and hit the wagon and turned it back into them. They were dead before they hit the ground. It damn near cut them in half."

Lucas didn't know what to say to the old man. He didn't know if he should tell him what had happened to he and Cyrista on the way home today or not. He decided not to say anything. If Cyrista wanted him to know, she would tell him herself.

"You have a lifetime full of pain and heartbreak," Lucas said as he walked over to the old man. "What keeps you from going off?"

The Ancient One broke into a small smile, "Time, Rider. Time is the answer. Time is the only thing that will heal the heart; time is what we all need to ask the right questions and come up with the right answers. You must count your blessings, Rider, no matter how small you think they are. You play a bad hand good and you can win. You play a good hand bad and you can lose. I've always tried not to put time limits on things in my life.

"I may have had too short a time with my Mary and my boy, but the way I see it, I was blessed to have any time at all with two of the most wonderful people that the good Lord saw fit to put here on Earth. And

He gave that time to me. You understand what I'm telling you, Rider."

Lucas was standing close to where the Ancient One was sitting and extended his hand out to him. As they shook hands Lucas said, "Yes, sir, I think I do. But give me a little time and I'll understand it better."

The Ancient One let out a little chuckle and pulled Lucas down next to him, "Yeah, I'm sure you will.

"Come with me, there's something I want to show you."

They walked up the path to the back of the motel. "I don't disapprove of you and Cyrista. It's about time she found someone. She's been alone too long not to have a man in her life. Hell, all she does is work and look after my old crusty ass."

Lucas laughed then asked, "Is that what you want me to call you?"

"What's that?" the old man asked. "Old crusty ass? If you want my crusty ass foot up your smart ass." They both had a good chuckle.

Lucas thought for a minute and he didn't really know the Ancient One's name. "Well, since you put it that way I still don't know what to call you." Sure he knew that his last name was the same as his own: Payne, but what was his first name? "Mr. Payne?"

"Don't call me that!" the old man snapped.

"Well what the hell do you want me to call you? You've ruled out crusty ass and now you've ruled out Mr. Payne."

"Rider, look on your drivers license and you'll know what my name is. If you don't feel comfortable calling me your own name, call me Pap-Paw. Any questions?"

Lucas looked over at the Ancient One with a half smile and said, "I should have known that you and me would have the same name. We seem to share a lot, why not names?"

The Ancient One just smiled and put his island-sized hand on Lucas' shoulder.

They reached the shed on the far side of the motel. The shed was down on a flat a few yards down from the back of the last room on that side of the motel. It was old but well built and it had power running to it.

The Ancient One pulled his keys from the clip on his belt. The oversized door had three locks on it. When he had unlocked the last one he swung the large, thick door open. Lucas was surprised to see how much room was in the shed when the old man hit the light switch.

They walked to the far left corner of the shed. Lucas was several yards in tow. He was busy looking around in amazement; he felt like he had walked into a time warp.

Lucas turned to catch up with the old man just in time to see the unveiling of a dark red 1953 big bagger Indian Chief. It was perfect. Lucas just stood with his mouth hanging wide open.

"Close your mouth, Rider. I don't want you slobbering on my bike."

Lucas looked over into the smiling face of the old man; he acknowledged by closing his mouth and nodding his head. Slowly he walked over to the bike. When he got close enough to touch it he looked again to the old man as if to ask permission. Still smiling, the old man nodded his head in approval and Lucas found his tongue. "Holy shit, its perfect! It looks like she just came off the showroom floor."

"Not quite. Take a look at all the chrome. That's not stock. We took what we wanted off and sent them to a war buddy of my boy's and had them done. He was from your neck of the woods. Up Nashville way."

The old man shook out an old feather duster made from ostrich feathers. Slowly he dusted the small amount of dust that was on it. Lucas was standing close by and told him that he hadn't seen a bike like that since 1963; that his cousin who was quite a bit older than himself had one, but it didn't compare to his in the looks department.

For the next hour they played with it. The Ancient One primed her up and cranked it. It was sweet. He offered to let Lucas ride it, but Lucas would have nothing to do with that.

When they closed the door to the shed, Lucas felt like he was walking out of bike heaven. They walked together toward Lucas' room. When they reached the room, the old man very casually said, "Get your stuff and bring it up to the house."

"What?" Lucas asked, being caught off guard by the old man.

"You heard me. I'll give you a hand."

"Do I have anything to say about this?"

"Rider, the weekend is coming and I'll need the room. I'm booked for the next week. They've got a craft show in town and I have some people coming in who come every year. I've got plenty of room up at the cabin and I sure as hell don't want to suffer the wrath of Cyrista for throwing you out on your ass."

They were gathering Lucas' things when Lucas told the old man there was something he wanted to talk to him about. "You know, Cyrista and me have gotten very close in a very short time. I don't know how you feel about that."

"Rider, let me tell you something: Cyrista is a grown woman; she knows her heart. Let me tell you something that you don't know about her. She has two grown kids. One lives in Florida and the other lives up in Asheville. She's forty-two years old, Rider. I stopped trying to tell her what to do a long time ago."

Lucas sat down on the bed shaking his head. "Old man, you like to do that to me don't you?" he didn't wait for an answer. "You like to see just how hard you can shock me, don't you?"

"Yeah," the old man said under a laugh, "and that's my good side coming out."

They looked at each other and laughed. Lucas was still in shock, but he was really beginning to like the

Ancient One. "Okay, Pap-Paw," he said, hoping to shock the old man at least a little bit. "You know what they say: pay back is a bitch." This got no reaction from the old man at all.

When they got to the porch of the cabin, Lucas was more out of breath than the Ancient One. Cyrista came out to greet them. She put her arms around Lucas' neck and kisses him on the mouth. He had both of his hands full and could do nothing but kiss her back. This had been an eventful day and it wasn't over with yet.

"Here, Pap-Paw, let me take that. I've got Lucas' room ready." The old man just shook his head. Cyrista had been doing that for years, knowing what he was going to do before he did it. He had grown used to it over the years, but it still amazed him.

He took a seat in one of the high back rockers and began to rock and Lucas and Cyrista carried the bags to his room. Lucas followed behind Cyrista.

She had on a pair of cut off jeans that were cut high and hugged low on her hips with a loosely fitting halter-top. He watched her walking barefoot across the room with her long hair bouncing from side to side. He had not been this happy in a very long time. He was getting turned on just watching her walk.

They got to the room and set the bags on the floor. His back was to the bed. She had a big smile on her beautiful face. All of a sudden she jumped at Lucas knocking him onto the bed on his back. She kissed him long and passionately. When she was done she pulled her head back and said, "I love you, Lucas Payne, and I will be back to finish this later tonight," then she left the room.

Lucas arranged his things in his new quarters. It was a nice room; big and open with two oversized windows. The ceiling was high and an old ceiling fan hung from the tongue and groove woodwork. The floor and walls were made of cut cedar boards that fit perfectly. The Ancient One knew what he was doing when he built this place.

It was getting late and Lucas needed to get a game plan together for when he was to meet Cissy at the place on the map that she had given him that morning.

Lucas found Cyrista busy in the kitchen. "Can you join me and Pap-Paw out on the porch, baby?" he said to her.

"Sure. What's up, Lucas?"

"I need to tell you something that happened when I went to town this morning."

"Oh yeah, while I'm thinking of it: do we say anything about what happened to us on the ride home?"

"No, Lucas, let's keep that between you and me; at least for the time being."…."Lucas," she started. He stopped her.

"I know all about it, baby. Pap-Paw told me."

"What's with you calling him Pap-Paw?" she asked him.

"He told me to either call him Lucas or Pap-Paw, so to cut down on the confusion I thought it would be easier to call him Pap-Paw."

"How sweet, that big ol' softy…I'll be right out, Lucas."

Lucas went out on the porch where the old man was sitting. He found a rocker and sat down without saying a word. Cyrista came out shortly after carrying a tray with three glasses of tea on it and graceful served one to each of them.

Lucas wasn't sure how to begin telling them what had happened this morning at the café, so he just started and hoped they would pick up on it. "This morning when I went to town to call my brother I stopped and had breakfast at the little city café. A woman by the name of Cissy waited on me. She pointed out a man sitting at the counter that she said had asked about me. She went on to tell me to watch my back cause he was no account and he was 'tied up with them'. When I went to pay my check she handed this to me when she gave me my change."

Lucas handed the note with the little map drawn on the bottom to the old man. He studied it for a minute then he handed it to Cyrista. She looked at it for a second and then she angrily crushed it up between her hands. As she stood up she threw it on the floor. "Damn, damn, damn!" she repeated. "Now they've got Cissy."

Lucas sat there confused and said, "What do you mean they have her? She was trying to help me."

"That's exactly what they wanted you to think Lucas. It's a trap and you would have fallen right into it if you hadn't come to me and Pap-Paw with this. Thank God that you did, Lucas; tonight is a full moon. They have their biggest gatherings on the first full moon. You would have made a wonderful guest appearance for them tonight…I'm sorry, Lucas; I don't mean to snap at you…it's Cissy. I never would have thought that they could have gotten to her. We grew up together. She used to spend the night right here in this house."

"I'm sorry about your friend, Cyrista," Lucas said. "I'm glad that we all spent time together today and built the trust I have for you and Pap-Paw. Otherwise it might be my ass hanging out there tonight."

Lucas sat for a moment; then a little smile came to the right side of his mouth.

"What ya thinking about, Rider? Come on, say it. I may be old, but there's nothing wrong with my hearing. I can hear you thinking" the old man said.

Cyrista stood there looking from one to the other. She couldn't believe how tight they were. It was scary to see two men who were so much alike working together. At the same time, she loved it. She had never seen Pap-Paw take to anyone so much.

Lucas was smiling at both of them and said, "Let's have a little fun and give them a taste of their own shit. You know when and where they have their gathering, right?" They both nodded their heads. " How much time do we have before they start?"

Cyrista looked at her watch. "We've got about two and a half hours before they set their little trap for you and about eight and a half hours before they start the fire dance."

"Rider," the old man said, "I knew there was something about you that I liked."

"What do you need? If we don't have it, we'll get it"

Lucas gave them high fives and started the deployment. "I need two boxes of shotgun shells, some ten penny nails, and about twenty, three-foot sections of one by three boards.

The old man looked at Cyrista, "Baby girl, you know where the shells are. Get them and meet me and Rider down by the shed."

Cyrista gave Pap-Paw a big hug and kissed him on the cheek. It had been years since the old man had called her baby girl, and she hadn't seen that light in his eyes for just as long.

"Hey," the Ancient One yelled after her as she hurried off, "change your clothes. We'll be headed for the mountain side."

"Okay," she hollered back, not missing a step.

Cyrista showed up at the shed where Lucas and Pap-Paw had the works in progress. They had drug up a pile of one by three boards, which Lucas had over the sawhorse cutting them into three-foot sections while the old man was busy pounding the nails through them. Cyrista asked what she could do to help. The Ancient One told her to go get the pickup truck, bring it over, and start loading up the finished boards.

She was off and running. Lucas looked at what she had done. She looked like something out of a Soldier of Fortune magazine. She was wearing military style lace-up boots with fatigue pants bloused into the top of the boots and a shirt to match the pants. Her hair was pulled up under a black beret and she wore a belt with a military holster containing a .45 hanging from it.

Lucas stopped what he was doing and waited for the old man to finish pounding the last nail into the board. "Does she know how to use that thing?"

The old man smiled and said, "I sure as hell wouldn't want to be on the receiving end of it. Yeah, Rider, she's deadly, better than I ever was and she's not afraid to use it...especially on them."

"Rider, I think you oughta know that what you're going to see tonight would be funny if it wasn't so foul and sick. These animals will do anything and stop at nothing. They don't care for anything, not even themselves or their kind. Its like their minds have been taken...you'll see."

Cyrista pulled up with the truck and started loading up the finished boards. When she had finished she said, "We'd better hurry up or we'll get there too late."

"Don't worry," Lucas said, "we've got plenty of time.

They all stopped what they were doing. "Okay, here's the plan," Lucas began. "We get up to where they have the fire before any of them get there. We'll plant the shells up there and wait for all of them to gather, then we'll go down to where they all drive in and put the boards where they will do the most good...or should I say, the mast damage."

The Ancient One had been taking it all in when he added, "I'll drop you and Cyrista off. You go up on the mountain and take care of the fire site and I'll take care of the details with the exit plan for our friends."

Lucas was shaking his head and said, "Sounds like a plan to me. How about it, Cyrista?"

"Yeah, yeah. Whatever you and Pap-Paw say. I'm here to help and be where I can do the most good. Or, like you say, Lucas: the most damage."

They finished with the boards and loaded everything up. They headed toward the spot where Lucas was supposed to meet Cissy and her goons. As they passed the turn off, they looked to see if anyone was waiting for him. There was no sign of anyone. It was still an hour until sundown.

Pap-Paw went around the corner to a cut-off from the road. If you didn't know where it was, you would never have seen it. He pulled up the hill to a flat spot and turned the truck around. "I'll be waiting for you right here whenever ya come down."

Lucas shook hands with him and Cyrista kissed

him on the cheek. Lucas asked, "Do you want me to come back down here and help you with the boards?"

"No, Rider, I can handle that just fine. I'll wait for all of them to get up there before I start. You just take care of my baby girl."

Lucas looked at the old man, "Hell, she's the one packing; she'll be the one to take care of me." The old man agreed with Lucas.

Cyrista smiled and said, "You can bet your sweet ass on that."

Lucas laughed, saying, "That's what I'm doing." He looked over to the Ancient One and said, "We'll be down after the fireworks."

Lucas and Cyrista jumped out of the pickup truck and disappeared into the thick growth in a matter of seconds.

The climb started off very steep at first, then started to ease up the farther they went. Lucas followed Cyrista and was really putting out to keep up with her. At the halfway point Cyrista looked back to Lucas and saw that he had fallen behind. She waited for him to catch up and said, "Let's take five."

Breathing heavily he said, "No shit. It's about time. I didn't know that you were part mountain goat."

She waited for him to get seated before she handed a canteen of water to him. He set down the bag of shells and took it from her. After taking a big drink he handed it back to her and said, "Where did that come from? I didn't see you get it."

"How did you miss it? I had it right here on my belt," she said.

"I guess I wasn't looking at your belt. I was more interested in what's under it.

"Ya know, it's been a long day and it looks like we're in for a lot longer one yet to come. Being here with you and your Pap-Paw has been a good thing for me. It's been a long time since I've been able to trust people. The only one that I've trusted in years is still in prison." He hesitated before going on. "As you know, I was just recently released from prison. Trust is something I'm gonna have to learn again."

"Oh, Lucas," she said in a sad voice, "I knew that something was bothering you. I'm relieved. I thought it was me or something I did or said. It's all right, baby. I don't care where you've been or what you've done. Our lives began when you rode up to the motel a few days ago. Pap-Paw told me that you had something dark riding with you. You'll be okay. Ya just need a little time and we'll do anything that we can to help. You're not alone anymore, baby: only when you want to be or need to be. Everything will be all right. You'll see."

They continued their climb upward. Lucas had no problem keeping up this time. He felt as if he had left a heavy backpack where he and Cyrista had talked. He was thankful for having met such good people. He knew he would have to relax a little more and be more trusting, which had never been an easy thing for him to do.

When they got closer to the top, Cyrista signaled for Lucas to stop. Together they quietly moved to a clearing. Lucas was surprised how big it was. It must have been at least four or five acres. They sat still for a few minutes looking and listening. No one was up there.

"This is a great spot," Lucas said to Cyrista. "I didn't think it would be so big and well kept. How many of them come up here?"

"Well, tonight is a special night," she said, "there will be close to two hundred."

"Holy shit!" Lucas exclaimed. "I never thought there would be anywhere close to that many."

"Let's get done with what we came up here for. We'll have plenty of time to talk while we wait for the show to begin."

Lucas was moving out to the direction of the large, burned out spot where they built their fires before Cyrista could say anything. He reached the spot and quickly pulled out his K-bar and started making holes in the ground behind the ashes. Cyrista came up behind him with the shells and placed them into the holes and gently covered them. When they had buried the last of the shells, Lucas found a branch and moved it over the entire area to cover the evidence that they had been there.

They had no sooner finished their chores than they heard the sound of trucks coming up the mountain. Without hesitation they shot toward the cover of the brush. As they dove into the edge of the brush and the small growth of trees, the trucks came into the clearing. Lucas motioned for Cyrista to follow him. Keeping low to the ground, they crawled deeper into the cover of the bigger trees.

The trucks made a circle around where the fire was to be built. There were four of them in all and they were full of wood for the fire. The first truck was stacked high with small branches and brush to get the fire started, so that truck was unloaded first.

They were making plenty of noise now, so it would be safe for Lucas and Cyrista to talk. "That was close," Lucas said as he huddled down close to Cyrista.

"Yeah," she replied under her breath, "too damn close."

When they had finished unloading the first truck, they all grabbed a beer from a cooler and gathered around the tailgate of the empty truck. They were talking and laughing but Lucas and Cyrista could not make out anything that was being said.

After they had unloaded two more of the trucks, they pulled the last one off a good distance from the fire site and unloaded it there. The wood for the fire was piled high. It would be one hell of a fire. There was enough wood to burn well into the next day.

The wood haulers once again gathered around the last truck to drink a beer. They were closer now to where Lucas and Cyrista were hiding; their words were now audible to the two. They weren't saying anything of importance. If Lucas didn't know better, he would have thought that they were a bunch of good old country boys making ready for a good ol' party in the country.

The sun was going down behind the mountain and the shadows were getting long. The wood haulers were getting ready to move out. They were careful not to litter. One of the boys got a big, black trash bag out and the rest of them put the beer cans into the bag.

Another truck was pulling up now. When it got to where the wood haulers were, three big, rugged looking men got out. Lucas recognized one of them to be the man at the cafe that morning.

Now Lucas and Cyrista could hear every word being said. The driver said, "That little squirrelly bastard never showed up. Man, I hate that. I sure had a few tricks that I was going to show the little son-of-a-bitch."

"Yeah, me too." Said another one.

Lucas was smiling and in a very low voice said to Cyrista, "Yeah, the trick is on them tonight." Cyrista squeezed his hand and smiled back at him.

A car was pulling up behind the last truck that had come. Cyrista jabbed Lucas and told him that it was Cissy's car. Two men got out of the car, but there was no sign of Cissy. The two men were laughing and the driver said, "Y'all should've seen that little wild cat. I finally had to hit her in the head." They all got a big laugh from that.

The man that had been at the café that morning asked, "Where is the little shit?"

"In the trunk," replied the driver.

The driver walked around to the back of the car and opened the trunk. He bent over and pulled out a big gunnysack, which he then dropped to his feet. After he closed the trunk, he dragged the sack around to the front of the car. "We'll still have our fun tonight," he said in a loud, laughing voice. Several of them laughed and encouraged the idea.

The big man from the café said, "Let's get a movin' boys. Slick, you stay and watch over that, there possum in the sack." Several of the men took the trucks and Cissy's car to the far end of the clearing and left them there. They climbed into the other pickup trucks and headed down the mountain. They were driving like a bunch of teenagers; spinning out, sliding, throwing dust up into the air and yelling like wild men.

The one they called 'Slick' sat there and finished off his beer. He looked over at the large sack. Whatever, or whoever was in the sack was moving now. Lucas and Cyrista both figured that it was Cissy in the sack, judging by the size of it. They had decided to use Cissy tonight, since Lucas was a no-show.

Cyrista motioned for Lucas to follow her, but Lucas held up a finger to wait a minute. The guard, Slick, was standing up. He moved to the sack and bent over. He said something that Lucas and Cyrista could not quite hear. Still bent over, he grabbed the middle of the sack and set it up. He moved around to the front of the sack and untied it. Cissy's head popped out of the top of the sack. She was gasping for air and crying. There was blood running down the left side of her face from her head and, from what Lucas and Cyrista could tell, it was flowing pretty good.

Lucas motioned for Cyrista to follow him. They moved slowly and quietly out of hearing range. "Oh, Lucas, I don't know how she got tied up with those animals, but we have to help her. She's hurt bad, but I fear she'll be worse off than that if we don't."

Cyrista was almost in tears. Lucas grabbed both her hands and shook them. "All right," he said, "but you have to get a grip."

"Okay," she said, "She's one of my oldest and best friends. We can't leave her for those beasts."

It was getting dark and Lucas knew that they didn't have any time to waste. "Cyrista," he said, "we don't have a lot of time. The rest of the pack will be coming up that road any minute now. You have to trust me and do exactly what I say. Do you understand?"

"I understand, baby, and I trust you with my life."

"That's good, cause that's what's at stake here. Now, first thing, if you don't have one in the chamber, put one in and follow me."

She pulled the old .45 from the holster and slid a round into the chamber as she followed close behind him.

They made their way around to where the road was and stopped. Lucas pulled his shirt off and then his 'Serenity' T-shirt that Cyrista had given him. He told her to use it like a bandana and make sure that all of her hair was covered. "Anyone that has seen you would remember that hair," he said. "I don't think this ass-hole guarding Cissy has ever seen me before. Walk in back of me a few steps and stay in my shadow."

Lucas quickly put on the shirt and Cyrista's beret. He opened up the cotton sack that the shells had been in and put in a rock the size of his fist. He kissed Cyrista and asked her, "Ready, baby? It's show time."

They came out onto the road just out of view from where Slick was guarding Cissy. He had his back to them. Lucas couldn't tell for sure, but it looked like Slick was standing over Cissy and pissing on her. What a sweet guy this one was. He could hear Cissy crying and Slick laughing as they got closer.

"Hey!" Lucas yelled at Slick's back.

Slick turned and said, "Hold em up right there. What ya'll doin'?"

Lucas didn't stop, but he answered Slick, "This is where the meeting is tonight?" He was still moving toward Slick but didn't give him time to answer. "Our damn truck quit on us coming up that road there." He was getting close and could see that Slick looked like he was a mental midget. He just stood there looking stupid with his mouth open and his dick in his hand.

Lucas was glad to see that such a dumb ass had been left behind to guard Cissy. Lucas was now almost in striking range, but he always liked having an edge; and this inbred looking freak gave him one. Lucas pointed and said, "Put that thing up, lessen ya aim to shoot me with it."

Slick looked down and began to laugh when Lucas hit him hard with the rock. Blood squirted out from the side of Slick's head hitting Lucas and Cyrista both. His feet flew up in the air and he hit the ground hard. He was out cold, maybe even dead. Lucas had hit him harder than he meant to, but he wanted to make sure this brain dead son-of-a-bitch didn't give him any trouble. Slick had also done a good job of pissing Lucas off by pissing on Cissy like that.

Cyrista and Lucas looked at Cissy. Her head was still bleeding. She looked up at them and said, "Oh, thank God." She was squinting her eyes, trying to focus on them. Then it hit her who they were.

Cyrista ripped the bandana off her head and tore it from top to bottom in the front. As Lucas took out his K-bar and started cutting Cissy out of the bag, Cyrista tied the shirt around Cissy's head to try to stop the bleeding.

"Cyrista," Cissy said.

"Shut up and do as you're told," Cyrista snapped.

"Can you walk?"

"Yeah."

Lucas looked over at Cyrista as he cut the leg ties. He was a little surprised because he hadn't seen this side of Cyrista before. Lucas checked on Slick; he was still alive. He figured Slick didn't have enough brains in his head for a headshot to kill him.

Lucas looked at Cyrista. She looked back at him, and with much concern in her voice she said, "She's lost a lot of blood, Lucas; she needs a doctor."

He looked over to where the trucks had been parked and then he looked down at Slick laying there bleeding. He reached into Slick's pocket and pulled out a set of keys. Running as fast as he could toward the trucks, he saw headlights coming up the hill. There were three trucks parked and he didn't know which one belonged to Slick. Lucas picked out the rattiest looking one and jumped in. He had picked the right one; the key fit and it started right up.

Lucas made a U-turn he heard a shot, then another. A truck was coming at Cyrista and Cissy but it turned hard to the left. Lucas wasn't more than ten yards from it when the driver door was opened up. Lucas turned the wheel and charged toward the door. WHAM! He hit it hard and the door was closed. It would take a torch to open that door again. He threw the truck into reverse and backed off. Then he moved his truck between them and Cyrista. Just as he was getting on it, there was a blast blowing out the passenger window. Glass flew all over the cab of the truck hitting Lucas.

Cyrista had Cissy up on her feet but she was leaning hard on Cyrista. Lucas pulled up and opened the driver side door and told Cyrista to hand him the gun. He threw it onto the seat and grabbed Cissy, pulling her into the truck. The back window was blown out. "This is getting old real quick," he yelled to Cyrista.

Lucas had Cissy in the truck now and yelled at Cyrista to drive. "Baby, drive!" Lucas grabbed up the .45 and put two shots into the windshield of the other truck. Those two good old boys were doing the get down now.

"How are you doing, girl?" Lucas asked Cissy.

"Better, now that ya'll are here."

Cyrista was driving the hell out of the old pickup as she made her way down the mountain. The road was narrow and there would not be room for two vehicles to get by each other. She made a sharp curve to the right when the headlights from an oncoming truck appeared.

"Hold your own, baby!" Lucas yelled above the noise of the engine and the wind blowing in.

Cyrista was smiling; she was enjoying this. She yelled to Lucas, "hold Cissy and brace yourself; this is going to be close." She had a death grip on the steering wheel of the old truck.

The truck coming up the mountain was almost

at a standstill, but trying to move closer to the side and out of Cyrista's way. Their bumpers clicked, then mirrors from both trucks crashed as Cyrista drove down the side of the truck without slowing down, but speeding up.

Lucas and Cyrista were both laughing hard and loud. Lucas yelled above the noise, "Go, girl, go! You're the greatest."

They were nearing the main road when they both saw a line of cars and trucks trying to turn in from both directions. "Oh, shit," Lucas yelled. The road was a bit wider at this point but still very narrow, and up ahead was a big dip. Cyrista ordered Lucas once again to hold Cissy then put the peddle to the floor. When she reached the top of the dip, the truck was airborne. A small car was coming up from the other side, but the truck went right over the top of it and came crashing down onto the pavement. The old truck bounced hard and slid into the side of another truck.

Cyrista didn't let up on the pedal one bit. The truck was spinning out, but when it caught it shot forward. Cyrista was all over the steering wheel but couldn't get the old truck straightened out in time and they hit one of the trucks in line to turn. She pulled the truck out of the crash and hammered it again.

Lucas was having the time of his life. He yelled to Cyrista, "Go, baby, go! Drive this mother!"

"Lucas," she said as she looked into the rear-view mirror, "we've got a little company."

Lucas turned to see two trucks coming up fast from behind. "Don't worry, baby," he said as he brought up the .45. "I'll handle this one. I'll get rid of them before we get to the turn-off where Pap-Paw is waiting."

Lucas turned sideways, waiting for the time being. When the lead truck got close enough, he stuck his arm out where the back window had been. He squeezed off two rounds into the grill, he dropped one low hoping to hit the steering tire, and then quickly put the last one into the windshield for good measure. The truck was about to hit their rear when it skidded sideways causing the one trailing to collide with it.

Lucas kept looking back, but all he could see was a big cloud of dust and smoke as they turned the corner. Cyrista let off the gas and glanced over at Lucas. She was still smiling. He was laughing and said, "That ought to keep them busy for a while."

Cyrista braked hard and turned into the little spot where Pap-Paw was waiting. She jumped out and told Pap-Paw to scoot over; that there had been a change in plans. Lucas came running around the back of the truck with Cissy in his arms. Pap-Paw opened the door and Lucas handed Cissy to him. Lucas closed the door and they were moving. Lucas jumped into the back of the truck as Cyrista pulled out.

As they got to the road, Cyrista looked to make sure that the coast was clear before she turned on the lights. Lucas leaned over and told Pap-Paw not to let Cissy go to sleep with that head wound. Pap-Paw acknowledged and cradled the frail little girl in his big arms. He was wiping the blood from her face and you could see that his big heart was breaking.

Pap-Paw had taken charge now. "Cyrista," he said as he looked up from Cissy, "go to the cross mountain road. We'll stop at old Doc Pickett's place and get this child fixed up."

The ride to Doc Pickett's seemed to take forever, and it seemed even longer to Lucas sitting in the back not knowing where they were going. When they finally pulled up in front of old Doc's house, a porch light came on and the Doc stepped out on the porch. He recognized the truck and yelled down from the porch, "That you, Payne?"

"Yeah," Pap-Paw answered. "We got us a little girl here with a big gash in her head." Lucas had jumped out of the back as soon as the truck had stopped and he opened the door and offered to take Cissy from Pap-Paw, but he would have nothing to do with that.

Little Cissy looked like a baby cradled in the big arms of the old man. When they reached the top step of the porch, old Doc Pickett was holding the door open. He looked at Pap-Paw and said, "Come on, come on, Payne. The girl will bleed to death as slow as you're movin'."

"Ha!" Pap Paw said. "I should have known better than to bring her up here to you. If ya do fix her up she'll jump off the side of the mountain once she takes a look at you."

"Put her down on the bed over in that corner," the old Doc said. "Turn on that light and turn off that big mouth of yours."

Cyrista looked over at Lucas and told him that they were always like this; that Doc Pickett was retired but he and Pap-Paw were very old friends.

Pap-Paw went over to where Cyrista and Lucas were standing. He told them to head to the kitchen and he followed. When they reached the kitchen and got under the light, Pap-Paw looked at Lucas and said, "Rider, ya look like hell. Are you okay, son?"

"Yeah, I'm fine," Lucas told him. He went over to the window and in the reflection he could see that the whole right side of his face was covered with blood. Cyrista took one look at his face and called him over to the sink. She started running cold water and she reached into a drawer and got out a clean towel. She started to clean his face but he took the towel from her and wiped away a nice splatter of blood from her face. She took the towel back and started to clean him up.

Pap-Paw went closer to the sink where Cyrista was cleaning Lucas's face and said, "You two must have had quite a time up there." Cyrista began telling Pap-Paw what had happened when Lucas flinched back in pain. She placed a chair under the light and told Lucas to sit in it so she could see what it was.

She put more water on the towel and slowly wiped above and to the side of his right eye.

"Hmmm," she sighed, "I see what it is." She left the room and came back with a pair of tweezers. She was in charge now. "Lucas, tilt your head. Pap-Paw, turn that light so it will shine over this way." Both men obeyed her orders. Slowly she pulled out four pieces of safety glass from the side of Lucas's head. When she had finished she put the clean part of the towel on it and told Lucas to hold it until she came back with alcohol and a couple of band aides.

Cyrista finished up with Lucas and said that she was going to see if Doc needed any help. When she had left the room Lucas asked the old man, "Do you think the old Doc's got anything to drink around here?"

The old man smiled at Lucas and said, "I'll bet I can find us one."

He walked over to the cabinet and pulled two small glasses and a bottle of George Dickel down. He poured one for Lucas, but before he could pour himself one, Lucas had slammed his down and had his glass back for more. "I think ya needed that, Rider," the old man said as he took a drink from his own glass.

"Yeah, I did. It got pretty intense up there for a minute or two. We almost didn't get the girl out of there in time. If we had been just a minute later, they would have had a trio entertaining them tonight.

The Ancient One put his hand on Lucas's shoulder and patted him. "I knew that I could count on you, Rider."

"Thanks," Lucas said. "But I couldn't have done it without your granddaughter. She's one hell of a woman."

The Ancient One raised his glass, "I'll drink to that." They clicked their glasses together and drank down what they had left.

"Where'd all that blood come from, Rider? That little bit of glass didn't cause all that bleeding, and Cyrista had some on her too."

Lucas smiled at the Ancient One and began. "They left one dumb inbred looking freak up there to guard Cissy. Well, Cyrista and me moved around to the road and walked up to him. I gave him the rock in the sock treatment upside the head. I hit him a little harder than I meant to. It split his head open good. I heard them call him Slick."

"I know who that is," The old man said. "That's old Slick Wilson's boy. It would have to be. They were always trash."

Cyrista and Doc walked into the kitchen. The Ancient One walked to the cabinet and got Doc a glass and poured him a drink while the Doc washed his hands. "Thanks, Payne," he said. : She took a good kick, went deep, clean to the skull. She'll be okay, but she needs to stay put for the night. She's restin' good and will till mornin'."

Lucas was and had been wondering: what of the law? Surely the sheriff patrol or state cops would be on this after the mess that was made on the road, He was certain that the Ancient One would know what the score on this was.

Old Doc Pickett sat down at the oak table and let out a big long sigh of frustration or relief. Lucas didn't know which one, nor did he think the Doc knew. Old Doc looked to the Ancient One, "It was those bastards again, wasn't it, Payne?"

The old man poured another glass from the bottle and stared into it for a second before answering. "Yeah, Doc, it was them alright. They've grown. It's no longer just a small band of freaks. Hell, man, they will have up to two hundred or more there tonight."

Old Doc hung his head and shook it back and forth. "What's to be done Payne? How did this get so out of hand?"

The Ancient One drank down the whiskey and said, "Time, Doc. Time has let this happen. Everyone around here thought I was crazy, including you.

"If it's any consolation to ya, Doc, Rider here made them pay tonight."

Doc looked over at Lucas and asked, "Who is this young feller anyway?"

The Ancient One got a little crooked smile because he knew that when he introduced Rider by his real name it was going to ruin old Doc. "This here is Lucas Payne, Doc."

Lucas stuck out his hand to shake Doc's, who was a little slow putting out his hand, but it finally met Lucas's. "My pleasure, Doc," Lucas said as he vigorously shook the Doc's hand.

The Ancient One was having a good time with this now. He would sit back, wait and watch what the old Doc would do or say next. Doc knew that he had been set up and he would be damned if he would let the Ancient One get the best of him. Finally he said, "It's good to meet ya, Lucas."

Cyrista was the one to come to Doc's rescue, "No relation, Doc. If it is, it's very far removed. He does kinda favor Daddy, doesn't he?"

Doc was getting his composure back, "Yeah…yeah, he does at that." Doc looked over at his old friend and snarled. He knew the old man had gotten the best of him.

Doc told them that he was going to go check on his patient. He left the room talking to himself under his breath. The Ancient One was smiling from ear to ear. "I hate to interrupt your victory," Lucas said, "but I have to ask you a question."

The Ancient One, still gloating said, "Anything, Rider. Anything at all."

"We left a pretty good mess up there on the road and on the mountain tonight. What about the law? Are they going to be up there and are they going to be after Cyrista and me?"

"Rider," the old man began, "The law has been

bought and paid for. If they do show up, those dirty bastards will simply tell them to go home.

"No, Rider, don't worry about a thing. They won't be after you. But I'll tell you one thing: you're in this thing deep. They'll never let you rest now. No matter where you go, they'll be looking. They've got the money and resources to find you too. They have what used to be good, decent people and somehow brought them into their evil circle. People from all walks of life."

Lucas held onto every word that the Ancient One had said. He was relieved to hear that the law was out of the picture. The last thing he needed was to go back to prison. Now all he would have to is figure out what to do about all the sick bastards that were now going to be after him.

Lucas glanced over at the clock on the wall. It was only nine-thirty, but it seemed a lot later. It had been a long, eventful day and it wasn't over yet. "Let's get some air," Lucas said, addressing both Cyrista and Pap-Paw.

Lucas sat on the top step and Cyrista sat next to him and put her hand on his leg. Lucas broke the brief silence. "We started something tonight and we need to finish it. I want to go back up on the mountain and watch the fireworks that we set for them. And we haven't put the boards out for the finishing touch. As long as I'm pissing people off I'd like to do a good job of it and at least have the pleasure of seeing it."

Lucas leaned up against the post and waited for a reply. The Ancient One spoke up, "Tell you what, Rider: we'll ride by and see if anyone is on lookout, and if there isn't, we'll finish up our night's work. Is that all right with you?"

"Sure thing," Lucas said with a smile.

Chapter Five

The crowd was steadily growing larger. Everything was done with a military precision. The cars and trucks were parked in the back corner of the clearing, packed in tight to accommodate the big turn out. The small campfires and tents were going up everywhere.

Tess and Terry were pleased, except that Lucas had not showed up as they had planned, but the son-of-a-bitch made off with their second offering. He would pay for this. Both of them had made a vow to make him pay.

The ceremony was minutes from beginning by the time Cyrista and Lucas got into position. Tess and Terry were standing on top of the scaffolding that had been erected for the occasion. Both of them were wearing long, black, shiny silk robes and their long, black hair was blowing slightly in the soft, warm breeze.

All at once they held up both arms and in a matter of seconds the only sound to be heard was the rustling of leaves as the crown spread out all around the fire site. Everyone was looking up to where Tess and Terry stood.

Terry started in a language that Lucas had never heard before. She went on for a few minutes then there was total silence. Lucas poked Cyrista a quietly said, "What was that supposed to be?"

In a teasing manner she said, "What, you can't understand what your girlfriend was saying?"

Lucas got red in the face and said, "Don't even go there; that's not even funny."

Cyrista had her little chuckle and said, "Okay, that's the last of that. I couldn't resist it one time.

"It's some kind of tongue they talk in…they were calling on the devil."

It was Tess's turn now. She started by saying, "Welcome each and every one of you. We are very pleased to see so many of you." Now both of them joined together and said, "Welcome sister witches and brother pagans. This is a time to celebrate." Then Tess alone continued, "We are growing. Our power is growing and we are becoming many, but together we are one." The sisters raised their hands up in fists and the people followed suit and began to cheer. The cheers grew louder then turned into a chant led by Tess and Terry. Lucas had no idea what was being said, but it went on for a good five minutes.

The chanting stopped as quickly as it had begun. Speaking together again the sister's said, "Let it begin." At the same time they both opened and dropped their robes. Everyone in the crowd did the same. Saying something in their strange tongue, they all joined hands and pointed to the wood piled on the fire site.

A flash came from their joined hands and hit the pile of wood with a big boom. The fire caught and the flames jumped high. "Pretty good trick," Lucas said. "But just wait a minute; I think our trick will be much more amusing." Lucas and Cyrista laughed and then both of them settled back to watch.

Seeing this from his safe hiding place, Lucas couldn't help but thinking how the first white man must have felt when he saw the Indians dance around a fire. It probably scared the hell out of him. This was even better than that…men and women alike, totally naked dancing wildly as if they were possessed.

This was a spectacle that Lucas would not soon forget. This was a wild bunch. Lucas had been to some pretty crazy biker parties where things got pretty wild, where a wet T-shirt contest would turn into a totally nude contest, but it was kept to a level. These people seemed to have no limits. They were taking a dead cat now and sharing its blood. Off in the shadows were two men and two women having sex. It didn't take but a few minutes for them to be joined by six other people. Things were wild and Lucas had seen enough. It was time to get down and meet Pap-Paw anyway.

Lucas motioned for Cyrista to follow him. They hadn't made it more than three feet when it happened. The first of the shells went off. Some of the people stopped and looked, but most of them just kept on with the party. Lucas and Cyrista stopped. They knew it would only be a few more seconds until all hell broke loose.

When the other shells went off you would have thought that the devil himself were coming out of the fire. Five or six of them went off at once. Sparks flew twenty feet above the fire. Hot cinders were flying all around the fire dancers, hitting their naked bodies. More shells blew. This was getting good. Nobody knew which way to go; they were running all over each other. All the time more shells were going off, adding to the dilemma.

Lucas was laughing so hard that he couldn't have moved if he had to. So many people had run into the scaffolding that it was about to turn over. Tess and Terry were holding onto the poles on the backside of it, helping it to lean more. Then it went. It landed on top of four or five people. Tess and Terry went flying and landed on top of a big fat man, driving him to the ground. The man grabbed one and rolled on top of her. Lucas figured that he thought it was a gift from heaven. It was too much; things had turned out better than Lucas had hoped.

Lucas didn't know how it had happened, but someone went running across the open field with hot cinders glowing from their ass. Running and screaming, trying to get the cinder off his ass, he hit a tree with full force. Cyrista and Lucas could hear the thud when he hit.

Cyrista turned to Lucas. It was her turn to split a gut laughing. "I'll bet that hurt," she said. "Oh, Lucas, this is great. I wish I brought a video camera. We could get rich selling this stuff."

It was hard for them to leave. Every time they thought that the shells were all spent, one or two more would go off. They turned and headed down the mountain, laughing with every step.

Most of the fire dancers had moved away from the fire and were headed to their cars or tents. Only the wounded and those helping the wounded were left close to the fire. If any of the dancers wanted to leave the mountain tonight it would take a while to untangle the mess because of the way they had parked their cars and trucks so close together. What a night it had turned out to be. A person couldn't buy that much fun.

Pap-Paw was right on time. He came around the corner at the same time Lucas and Cyrista reached the pavement. They jumped into the seat, both of them still laughing. Pap-Paw looked at them and said, "It must have gone well by the way you two are carrying on."

Cyrista was beside herself, "Oh, Pap-Paw, it was great! I wish you could've seen it." She went on telling him every detail of the incident. Before they got back to the motel, Pap-Paw was laughing as hard as they had been.

"Rider," Pap-Paw said, "I'll go unlock the shed and you get your bike and bring it down here tonight. We'd better be safe tonight. There's no telling what they might do since y'all crashed their party."

The old man drove down to the end of the motel where the shed was. By the time he got the door open, Lucas was there and drove his bike into the shed.

The three of them started their walk up to the cabin. A few of the guests were about and stirring, enjoying the night air. Pap-Paw and Cyrista exchanged pleasantries with a few of them along the way.

"Damn, I'm hungry," the old man said.

"Yeah, me too," added Lucas.

Cyrista looped her arms into each of theirs and said, "Well, come on. I'll feed my hungry men. You've both earned it."

It had been a long time since Lucas felt like he belonged. It felt good to him to fit in somewhere after having lived his whole life like an outsider. Very few people had ever known the real Lucas Payne because of the wall he put up, but it was different with these people. He had a real connection here, but he was worried for the safety of his new friends, and for his own.

The two men went in and washed up as Cyrista went into the kitchen, then Lucas and Pap-Paw went out on the porch to relax for a while. The next thing Lucas knew, Cyrista was gently waking him up. He looked around for Pap-Paw, but he was gone. "Come on in, baby. Come in and eat a little something."

He walked into the kitchen. The Ancient One handed him a cold beer. "Thanks," he said. "I must have dozed off for a minute. You all have me worn out today." He looked at the table where he saw a big pile of fish left over from lunch, fresh garden tomatoes sliced just right and a batch of hot hush puppies. He took a long pull off the cold beer and dug in.

By the time they finished the late meal they were ready for sleep. Lucas still had one question for the old man though. "Where does this evil come from and why does it have to be here? I just don't understand. This area is as close to heaven as one can get."

"Evil," he said, "does not exist without good. It is in the eye of the beholder what is good or evil."

"Sometimes when good faces evil, it becomes evil to exist, but no evil is ever good. That may sound like a bunch of double talk, but think about it. To answer your second question of why it is here. Well, I believe it came here a long time ago. When evil is in a place, it draws evil to it and grows like a cancer."

"Now, I'm going to bed. Goodnight child; goodnight, Rider." They both bid him goodnight and he was off to bed.

Cyrista walked up in back of Lucas and began rubbing his shoulders. "He is a wise old man, Lucas. Sometimes it's hard to understand his wisdom, but give his words time and they'll make sense."

"No, no, Cyrista," Lucas said, "I understand what he said. I just never thought of it that way before. It makes sense now that I've heard it."

Lucas woke the next morning to the sounds of the country. He felt like a new man. The night's sleep had been the best since he left Tennessee. The house was quiet; there were no sounds of anybody stirring about. He slipped on his pants and went to the kitchen. When he looked at the clock on the wall he was in disbelief that he had slept in so late. It was already eight-thirty.

The coffee was left on and two sausage biscuits sat wrapped for him next to his coffee cup. He fixed his coffee and sat down at the table. When he had finished his breakfast and stood up to go to his room for a smoke, he noticed the note that Cyrista had left him. He picked it up and read:

"Good morning, sleepy head.

I hope you feel better.

Pap-Paw and I had to run a few errands.

We'll be back in a few. Come down to the office when you get ready.

I love you Lucas Payne.

Love, Cyrista."

Smiling all the way to the bedroom he got his cigarettes and walked out to the porch. "Good morning, Lucas Payne." The soft little voice came from the far end of the porch. It didn't startle him, but it was a surprise.

"Cissy," Lucas said. "This is a surprise. How are you feeling?"

"Oh, Lucas, I'm so sorry for what I tried to do to you and…and…" She couldn't go on. She put her head down into her hands and began sobbing uncontrollably.

Lucas wasn't sure what to do at first. He was pissed at her for trying to set him up, but it did a total backfire on her. He figured that she had been punished enough.

He walked over to her and took hold of her hands. "That's enough of that shit. What's done is done. Hell, girl, you got the raw end of that deal. We'll start off fresh, but you'll have to earn my trust. You know the old saying: Screw me once, shame on you. Screw me twice, shame on me. There will be no shame on me."

"I owe you my life, Lucas. I'll do anything, anything at all. I'll never be able to repay you for what you did for me.

"I don't remember much; I was so scared. I just knew they were gonna kill me. If Cyrista wasn't your woman, I'd show you how much I mean what I'm saying. Cyrista told me everything you did last night. She said that you really got that animal, Slick Wilson. Did ya kill him?"

Lucas was looking at old Doc Pickett's handiwork. The stitches were small and tight. If the wound left a scar on that pretty head it would be a small one.

They were looking each other in the eyes and she said, "Please forgive me. I didn't want to set you up, but they forced me to."

Lucas wasn't sure that he wanted to hear or to know any more about her problem, but her problem reflected directly on him. They wanted him bad enough to go to some extreme to set him up. "Tell you what. Give me a chance to get a shower and wake up and I'll came back out, then we can talk. I'm not much of a morning person until I've had my shower and at least three cups of coffee."

He stood up to go inside; she stood up, put her arms around him and hugged him tight. "Thank you, Lucas. Thank you," she said, and took her arms down.

Lucas was thinking to himself: damn, I just got through telling her that I'm not a morning person, then she goes and does that. He turned and walked into the house without saying a word.

During his shower, Lucas got the urge to pack up and ride out of this place. If he changed his course a little, he could be in Florida not long after dark, and be drunk by eight or nine o'clock. But whom was he trying to fool? He could never in his life run from a fight, not to mention Cyrista.

He walked back out onto the porch with a fresh cup of coffee. "Yeah, I feel better now," he said as he sat next to Cissy. "I don't know if I killed Slick or not. It wouldn't be much of a loss to the world if I did, so it really doesn't matter. I don't think it killed him though. Scumbags like him for some reason seem to live long and shitty lives.

"What's the deal, girl? How did they force you to set me up?" He hated asking this question for fear that she would tell him the answer, and he wasn't sure he wanted to know. He was already in deep enough.

Cissy took a deep breath and started. "Do you remember the big, ugly man that I pointed out to you in the café?" Lucas nodded and she went on. "Well, that pig is my ex-husband. He used to be a wonderful man and that's why I married him. He was so kind and gentle. I had a little girl before him and me got hooked up, but he loved her like she was his own flesh and blood. Ya couldn't ask for a better daddy.

"He lost his job and started runnin' with that crowd. I could see the changes in him right away. He started getting mean an hateful. I thought that once he found another job he'd go back to the sweet, lovable man he used to be. Then, when he found a job, he just got worse. We fought all the time, then he beat me one night and damn near killed me. You know the rest of the story: restraining order, divorce, and all the mess that goes with it.

"He didn't bother us for two years. I would see him in passing every now and then; he even started coming into the café once in a while and we began to talk. He told me that he was getting help and he was sorry for what happened.

"A few days ago when I was getting off work, he came in and said we needed to talk. We went out to his truck and he told me that they had my baby and if I didn't do exactly as I was told that she would be dead. They had her all right, and they still do." Cissy started crying again, but finished saying, "I'm sorry, Lucas. I had no choice to do what I did. They want you bad, Lucas, real bad. They aim to kill you. Please, be careful."

This was getting crazy, but it put a whole new light on things. He stood up and looked down at Cissy. "I would have done the same thing in your place, Cissy. Don't feel bad about that; I totally understand. We have to deal with the problem at hand now.

"You stay up here and rest. I've got to go down and talk to Pap-Paw and Cyrista…you're safe here; don't worry."

Lucas's mind was rushing as he walked down to the office. What the hell else could happen? He was even feeling some guilt for what had happened to Cissy and her little girl. If he hadn't come this way and fallen in with those two bitches, none of this would have happened.

He quickly dismissed the "what if" bull shit. He had been through enough in his life to know better than to do that. What if always turn into what is. Almost all of last night's guests had checked out. The last ones were loading up their cars and preparing to leave. Pap-Paw was busy with the last customer, so Lucas went to look for Cyrista. He saw her coming out of room ten as he walked down the sidewalk. "Cyrista," he called to her.

She stopped and turned and, as usual, she had a big smile on her face as she came walking toward him. She put her arms around his neck and gave him a kiss. Somehow, no matter what was going on, she managed to keep her spirits up. Lucas admired that quality in her. Most women would be falling apart with what was going on.

"Good morning, you ol' sleepy head," she said in her cheerful tone. "It's a beautiful day, isn't it?"

Lucas just smiled and said, "It is now that I've seen you."

"You know just what to tell a girl, don't you, Lucas Payne?"

He hated to break the mood, but he had to. "Cyrista, I just had a talk with Cissy and she told me everything that happened. You, me, and Pap-Paw need to talk."

"I know. Help me finish up this last room here and we will.

"Have you ever heard anything so sad, Lucas? We're going to help her, we just have to figure out what to do."

They jumped in and quickly finished cleaning the last room. She amazed him. In the time it took him to strip the beds and changed the linens, she had vacuumed the floor, cleaned the bathroom, put up fresh towels, wiped everything down, opened the window, and was waiting for him by the pushcart.

They walked together, pushing the cart down the sidewalk. Pap-Paw was sitting outside the office enjoying the morning sun on his face. "Morning, Rider," he said.

"That was the best night's sleep I've had since I left Tennessee."

"That's good," the Ancient One said. "Lets go up to the house. I could use another cup of coffee. My little chicken there woke me up before the rooster crowed." He looked at Cyrista, winked, and smiled at her.

She reached down, grabbed his hand and helped him to his feet. "Come on, old man," she said as he stood up. He put his arm around her and they walked toward the cabin.

Lucas could see how close they were. They were family, but they were also best friends. She grabbed Lucas's arm and pulled him along with them. He felt good. He was happy, but something was warning him not to get too comfortable with it. With all of the garbage going on, something was bound to happen. Although he wanted to ignore it, he knew that he should listen. He would enjoy this as long as it lasted and do whatever he had to do.

Cissy was lying on the couch when they got up to the cabin. Pap-Paw went into the living room to check on her and Cyrista went to the kitchen to make coffee. Lucas stayed out on the porch to gather his thoughts and to enjoy the late summer's morning. He loved it here. He could see himself living here if only they could get through all of the bullshit that was moving in on them.

Cyrista brought the coffee out to the porch. Pap-Paw and Cissy followed behind her. When everyone was settled and had their coffee Pap-Paw spoke. "I've been thinking about this all morning. We have a delicate situation here. I've known Sheriff Dave Moss since he was a boy. Hell, I helped him get elected his first term in office. I trust him, but the last few years I've heard rumors that he's taking money to look the other way. Before we take these matters into our own hands, I want to go to him and put it on the line: cut and dry. At least that way we'll know where we stand. Is that agreeable with ya'll?"

Cyrista and Cissy were quick to agree, but Lucas had his reservations about anything to do with the law. He had known nothing but grief to come out of any dealings he had had with the law. "I can't say that I agree with you, but I'll go along with what you say," Lucas said. "This is your neck of the woods, not mine, so you should know what the score is. I'll back you up no matter what comes down."

"Thanks, Rider," the old man said. "I'm not sure if this is the right way to play this myself, but I think it's the best way to draw out who's who and cover our ass."

Pap-Paw made the call to the sheriff's office and told them who he was and that he needed to talk to the sheriff. The dispatcher knew the old man and told him that the sheriff was out on an emergency call. He said he would call him on the radio and tell him that he was needed. The dispatcher also told him that the sheriff was out that way, so it shouldn't be long.

Dave Moss was a round little man, a little shorter than Lucas. He wore no uniform and drove a four-wheel drive Ford Explorer. Lucas thought that he looked more like and old shopkeeper than a sheriff. When he reached the bottom of the steps to the cabin he greeted the old man. "Hello-lo, Mr. Payne. It's good to see ya, sir. How ya been feelin'?"

"I'm fine, Dave," the Ancient One said. "Why don't you bring your little, round ass up here and I'll talk to you instead of yelling up and down these steps."

"Yes, sir, Mr. Payne. I'm not as young as you are."

"No," the old man said, "but you're a hell of a lot rounder than I am."

Lucas was holding back his laughter. He could see who commanded the respect here. The round little sheriff held onto the railing, using it to pull himself up the steep stairs. By the time he got to the top he was breathing so hard that Lucas thought the sheriff was going to have a heart attack.

The sheriff sat down in one of the rockers and took off his hat. Sweat was dripping off of his head so he pulled out a handkerchief and mopped it up.

"Cyrista, darling, would you get Dave here some tea please? I don't want him to die up here on the porch. We'd have to carry him down and that would be a job."

Cyrista jumped up and headed to the kitchen. Lucas loved it. The old man had been digging at the fat little sheriff ever since he showed up.

"Dave, this here is a family friend of ours from Tennessee. We call him Rider."

Lucas stood up and shook hands with the fat little sheriff. "Good to meet ya, Rider."

"Likewise," Lucas said, not wanting to speak more than he had to. He liked the way the Ancient One introduced him to the sheriff. No name other than Rider and that he was from somewhere in Tennessee. The old man had style.

"How's business, Dave?" the Ancient One asked, not really expecting much.

"Well, Mr. Payne, its funny you should ask that. Ya remember old Slick Wilson? Well, some coon hunters found his body early this morning over by Tumbling Creek. Don't know what the boy was doin' down there, but by the look of things he had a pretty good fall. Had him a big ol' gash in the side of his head"

"The boys hauled him on outta there an up to the morgue. Well, bout nine o'clock old Mr. Phelps up at the morgue called me. Said young Slick ain't got no blood in his body. We got him up to the county coroner now seein' if they can figure anything out."

Lucas had gone stiff when the sheriff dropped Slick's name. He looked over at Cissy who had turned even whiter than she had been before. Cyrista had gotten up and moved around where the sheriff couldn't see her. Pap-Paw was cool. He didn't change his first expression. He just sat there and listened to Dave go on with his story.

"Well, Dave, that's too bad about the boy, but that's not why I called you up here today. This here little girl's baby has been taken and we know who's done the taken." The sheriff began to squirm a little and the old man went on. "It was her ex-husband and that group he's been running with. We want you to go up there and get her back and nothing will be said."

The sheriff was sweating profusely again; he wiped his head and got to his feet. Lucas could see where this was going and it was not good.

"How do ya know it was him that took the baby?" asked the sweaty sheriff. That was the wrong thing to say.

The old man got to his feet and in a very low voice he said, "you're not questioning my word, are you, Dave?"

"Oh, no, no…ah, Mr. Payne. I didn't mean it that way." The Ancient One looked like he was growing as he stood there. He was no longer slumped over; his shoulders were straight and broad. He looked like a giant standing there, glowering over the little man. Lucas had never seen anything like it. It was like Clark Kent turning into Superman.

"All I'm asking you to do, Dave, is go up there and check it out." The old man was cool. He didn't raise his voice or do anything else threatening toward the nervous little man before him.

"I, uh…I'm sorry, Mr. Payne, but I cant do that."

That was enough said. The Ancient One could

have burned a hole through him with the fire coming from his eyes. "I heard you'd gone yellow, Dave, but I didn't want to believe it. You used to be a good man, a fair man…what happened to you? Greed, Dave! Greed! You take that scum's money and leave decent folks out in the cold." Lucas was glad to be on the old man's side. He wouldn't want to be in the sheriff's place for anything.

The Ancient One wasn't finished with him yet. "Dave," he said in a much lower voice, "we're going to get the baby. Don't get in the way, 'cause if you do, I'll smash you like that fat little bug you are. Now get your fat ass off my porch before I throw you off."

The sheriff was moving now. About halfway down his stubby legs gave out and down he went. When he hit the landing he was up and running. The Ancient One was so mad that he was shaking. He took the coffee cup in his hand and threw it at the sheriff. It hit next to him and he squealed like a pig. That was it for Lucas; he couldn't hold back his laughter any more. He burst out and in a minute, everyone on the porch was laughing uncontrollably, including Pap-Paw.

In all the years Cyrista had been with Pap-Paw she had never seen him so angry. She too had witnessed the transition of him growing into a giant. She went over to where he was and put her arms around him. She stood on her tiptoes and kissed him. She had the power to make any situation better, no matter how bad it seemed. "Are you okay, Pap-Paw?" she asked.

He looked down at her and smiled. "I feel better than I have in twenty years. Damn, that felt good!

"Rider, lets you and me ride down and get a beer. I need two things right now and that's a ride on my bike and a beer."

Lucas looked at him a little surprised, then to Cyrista. She was smiling big and shaking her head, yes.

"Sounds like a winning combination to me," Lucas said. "I'm ready."

The Ancient One went to Cissy and gave her a hug and said, "Don't worry, child, things will work out. I promise you that. Me and Rider have got to put a plan together. You girls watch the fort and stay up here at the house.

"Cyrista, call Mr. Lee in to watch the desk for us. People will be coming in early today."

Pap-Paw walked to his bedroom. Cyrista said, Lucas, come here." She put her arms around his neck and said, "Ya know, you're pretty wonderful. I haven't seen him like this for a very long time. You bring out the best in us and I love you for it."

He gave her a big smile and pinched her on the butt and said, "I'll bring the best out of you later."

"You're bad, Lucas Payne," she said laughing.

Pap-Paw came out of the bedroom wearing dark glasses and an old bombers jacket. His long, white hair lay over the collar of the jacket, giving his look the finishing touch. He was carrying another jacket like the one he wore. "I want you to have this, Rider. It belonged to my boy, the other Lucas Payne."

For a moment Lucas choked up and couldn't say anything. Then the words came, "Thank you, Pap-Paw. I'll wear it with pride and honor." They shook each other's hands and the Ancient One told him to put it on. It looked good, just a little big, but not bad. It would give him room to put on more layers when the weather started to turn. The old man put his arm around Lucas's shoulders and they walked together.

They walked to the shed in silence. They both had a lot on their minds. Lucas knew that he would back up this old man no matter what. Especially after what Lucas had just witnessed between him and the little sheriff. This old man was no joke, and Lucas was proud to be with him.

After the old man went through his ritual of dusting the old Indian down, he primed it up, then kicked it twice and said something to it. He turned on the switch and kicked it one more time. Boom! She started right up. He let the Indian idle for a few seconds before revving her up. The old classic sounded great. It hit smooth, didn't miss a lick.

Lucas hit the starter. His old beast never missed, nine out of nine she started the first time. The Ancient One signaled for Lucas to follow. It was music to his ears following behind the old Indian.

They had a sound all their own; it was sweet. For a little while, Lucas forgot all his troubles.

They pulled up to a little bar on the far edge of town. They seemed not to be the only ones out for a ride on this beautiful day. There were three other hogs sitting out front where they parked.

They went inside. The door was left open. Lucas had always like a bar that left the front door open. It was kind of like saying that they had nothing to hide, come in and take a look. At the end of the bar were three bikers standing, just waiting to see who walked in.

A medium build man on the end was the first to speak. "Hey, Mr. Payne," he said in a cheerful tone. He turned to the guy standing closest to him and said, "Pay up, sucker."

The guy slapped a ten spot in his hand. The man turned to the bartender and said, "Give us a round, Sammy. Compliments of Jimmy Legs."

The Ancient One walked over to the three men. The guy that had ordered the round stuck out his hand to greet the old man. "I just bet Jimmy Legs here a ten spot when we heard your bikes pull up that it was you. I'd know that sweet sound anywhere. Good to see ya, Mr. Payne," said the man as they shook hands.

The Ancient One shook the hands of the other two, calling them by name. "Boys," he said, "this here's a family friend from Tennessee, just call him

Rider". Lucas extended his hand toward the one who'd bought the beers first. "This is Gus, that long-legged fellar is Jimmy Legs, and the big ole ugly one is Bad Billy." They all shook hands and drank their beers. They seemed to be good old boys as far as Lucas could tell from the first meeting.

After a little while, the Ancient One excused Lucas and himself. They walked to the back booth. "Rider, I've been studying on this problem that we've got. I haven't been able to think of any other way of dealing with it other than just going up there and facing the bastards."

Lucas took a long pull off the cold beer and said, "I reckon you're right. I've pretty much come up with the same thought."

They finished their beers and walked back up to where the other boys were. "What have you boys been up to? Been making any runs lately?"

Gus seemed to do most of the talking. "Ah, ya know, Mr. Payne, we ride when we can. Hell, I guess we ain't no different from any other sons-a-bitches: spend most o' the time workin' and the other time talking bout what we'd like to do."

"Yeah," the old man said, "then one day you turn around and you're an old man like me."

"Yeah, Mr. Payne," Gus said, "but ya still got yer face in the wind an that counts for a whole lot. Ain't much freedom left anymore; that's bout all we got left."

The Ancient One started thinking, "Rider, what do think about me asking these boys to go on a ride with you and me?"

"I think we should buy the next round," said Lucas. "You know these boys, not me."

"This here is on me, Sammy. Set us all up one more time." The Ancient One winked at Lucas and put a ten spot on the bar.

The three guys thanked him for the beers. Bad Billy raised his bottle and said, "to the coolest old rider that ever lived."

"Yeah, yeah, yeah," they all joined in together. It felt good to relax for a change. Lucas hit it off with the old man's biker buddies and bought them the next round. Everyone drank to a dying breed: the old biker.

It was Jimmy Legs that asked about Cyrista. The Ancient One told him that she was doing fine and that she and Lucas had a thing going. Of course, all the guys gave him shit after hearing this and called him a dog. Then they told him how lucky he was. They didn't tell him anything he didn't already know.

"Boys," the Ancient One started, "Me and Rider have a little problem." He went into the story, telling them everything. They all knew Cissy and liked her a lot. From what Lucas could tell, Bad Billy had a thing for her. He was ready to do anything that he could to help her. He also observed that these guys had no love for that bunch of "weirdos" as they called them, and they left no doubt that they would follow the

Ancient One to hell if he had asked them to go.

It was good to ride with a group again. It had been a long time since Lucas had done it. The ride to Cissy's ex-husband's house took about twenty minutes on the old mountain back roads.

They pulled up in front of the shack and killed their engines. There was no need to announce themselves. The boys at the shack had heard them coming a long way off. There were seven of them sitting outside on the porch and on the backs of pickup trucks. Lucas saw one inside peeking out the window, covering the others with a gun, he supposed.

"No need to pretend why we're here, boys," the Ancient One said to them. "Give us the little girl and there won't be any trouble; we'll just be on our way. The sheriff knows that we came up here."

All of the guys sitting around began roaring with laughter when the Ancient One said this. Lucas could see that it pissed him off. He had already learned that the old man was no nonsense when it came time to play the hand.

It caught Lucas totally off guard when the Ancient One reached behind his back and pulled out a Colt .45 and pointed it at the window. "All right you peeking little son-of-a-bitch, throw your shotgun out the door, now!" The Ancient One was not playing.

The man didn't react quickly enough to suit the Ancient One, so he squeezed off two rounds. The window shattered and the man inside said, "Don't shoot; please, don't shoot," and the shotgun came sliding out the door.

"You got till the count of three to get you stinking ass out that door." The old man counted, "One, two," Boom! Boom! Two more rounds went through the window. The man came out of the shack begging the old man not to shoot.

By this time, everyone was off the bikes except for the Ancient One. Lucas recognized a few of the guys on the porch as the wood haulers from the day before. He would never forget the big one that had dragged Cissy out on the trunk of her car in a big gunnysack. He had also been the one at the café that morning. Lucas figured that he was Cissy's ex-husband. He looked at the big, ugly man and said, "You, big brave man, get he girl now. We didn't come up here because we like ya."

The man smiled at Lucas and laughed. "Who do you think you are, you short little son-of-a-bitch?"

Lucas motioned for the Ancient One to put the gun away. The old man put it back in his belt behind him. Lucas started walking toward the man who stood up from where he was sitting. He was at least a foot taller than Lucas and a hundred pounds heavier.

Lucas kept walking toward him and the big man just stood there with his arms crossed, smiling at Lucas. When he was in striking distance he stopped. Looking up at the man, Lucas said, "You don't know me well enough to call me a son-of-a-bitch."

The big man laughed and dropped his arms. His arms had not even reached their full extent when, with lightening speed, Lucas came with a long over-the-head punch from the bottom. He put everything he had into the punch. When it connected, the big man's nose shattered all over his face. Lucas's feet came about a foot and a half off the ground and he stumbled forward as the big man went down. Lucas drilled him seven or eight times before the man hit the ground. This helped Lucas regain his balance. Blood had flown everywhere from the big man's nose and was pouring from it when his head bounced off the ground.

Lucas came around hard and quick, lifting his right leg as he did. He let go with a kick that caught one of the guys on the porch in his right eye. The guy's head went back, smacking a post behind him. He then slumped forward and fell to the ground.

Gus, Bad Billy and Jimmy Legs were all over the rest of the guys that had been sitting around. It was on. A few of the boys that had been there when it started had run off and were watching from a distance. They had lifted up their hands to the old man and said they had nothing to do with any of it. The Ancient One would not let them get into their trucks. He motioned for them to stand over where they had gone.

The fight didn't last long. The four riders made quick work of the bunch at the shack. Bad Billy was laughing and told the Ancient One that they would have to hang out more often. He hadn't had that much fun in a long time. They all laughed and agreed.

"Rider, go into the shack and see if you can find the girl," Pap-Paw ordered him.

"No problem," Lucas replied, as he turned to go inside. He looked into each room of the shack. Nothing. Nobody was there.

As Lucas came back out of the shack, Cissy's ex-husband was just getting to his feet. "She's not here and ya'll won't find her," he said.

"So far nobody's been seriously hurt," the old man said, "but that's fixing to change if I don't hear the right answers; and I mean now."

Cissy's ex was holding his nose and pointing at Lucas with the other. "Tomorrow night, you, and you alone come to the old Stanley place and you can have her."

"No way," the old man replied. "I'll be along with him. We're not stupid. Do you think we're going to let you kill us off one by one?"

"Whatever ya say, old man," he said, still holding his nose.

Lucas walked up to the big man and slapped his hand, the one holding his nose. He let out a big yell. Lucas looked at him and said, "That's for not respecting your elders." The rest of the riders got a good laugh from this.

"Come on, boys," said the Ancient One, "I believe

its my turn to buy. You've all earned it."

They cranked up and rode back to the little bar where the Ancient One called Cyrista and filled her in on what had happened. He told her to set three more plates for dinner; he would bring the boys with him. It would do them all some good to unwind and relax.

Back at the bar, the boys needed to unwind. Bad Billy said to Lucas, "Ya know, Rider, I've seen some fast old boys in my days, but you're faster than any I ever seen." Gus and Jimmy Legs both agreed.

The Ancient One interjected, "And hard-hitting too. Did you see the nose on that big dummy? It was all over his face. When you walked over to him and I saw how big he was, I was hoping that you had a plan."

Lucas took a long pull off his beer. He looked at the four men and said, "When that big old son-of-a-bitch stood up, I was wishing I'd stayed over by my bike. That mother was huge!"

All of them broke out in laughter. Jimmy Legs stuck out his hand to Lucas and said, "Ya got guts, man. You're okay in my book."

"Yeah, mine too," Bad Billy and Gus both put in.

"Boys, I can't thank you enough for the help you gave me and Rider. Let's have another round on me and then you're all going to ride with us back to my place. I've called home and got Cyrista and Cissy fixing up some groceries." This was all the old man had to say; Bad Billy's eyes lit up at the mention of Cissy. Gus and Jimmy Legs just looked at each other, smiled, and rubbed their hands together and made a yummm sound and laughed

Lucas liked these guys. He knew that they had character and that they were characters. Everyone finished their beer and each got six more to go. They loaded the beers up in Jimmy's trunk since he was the only one that had a big bigger. He didn't mind carrying the beer; he was used to it. The inside of his trunk had a thin liner of Styrofoam on the top, bottom, and sides.

Lucas looked to Jimmy Legs and said, "I know how you feel, Jimmy Legs. This used to have a tour pack on it and I was the one always carrying the beer.

"Look at the bright side of it: no one will leave you stranded on the side of the road."

"Ya got that right, Rider. Especially these beer hounds that I ride with."

Everyone was cutting up on the ride to the Ancient One's cabin. Their spirits were high and they probably hadn't had a home cooked meal in a while. They all parked in front of the office.

The hotel had filling up, just as the old man said it would. A small oriental man came running out of the office when the bikes pulled in. He was waving his arms and saying, "No, no, no park here…No park here!" Then he saw the old man and said, "Oh, so sorry, Mr. Payne. Lee not know it you…so sorry."

"It's okay, Mr. Lee. You're doing a good job."

They could see the smoke and smell the food from the parking lot, but before they went up to the cabin the Ancient One took Mr. Lee aside. He told him to keep a keen eye out and call if anything at all seemed unusual.

Mr. Lee had helped out at the motel for a very long time. It was he and Granny Franks that kept it going while the Ancient One searched the mountains for his beloved Mary.

Cyrista took one look at Lucas as he came through the door and said, "Well, Lucas Payne, you look like you had a very interesting ride. Come on in the kitchen and let me clean you up. This is becoming a habit with us."

Gus, Bad Billy, and Jimmy Legs all stood with their mouths hanging open. Jimmy Legs looked over to the old man and asked, "Did she just call him Lucas Payne?"

"Yeah," the old man replied. "It's a long story."

All three of the boys grabbed a beer and headed out to the porch. "This is getting very interesting," Gus said as they settled on the porch.

Cissy came out to check the burgers on the grill. Bad Billy got up and walked over to her. "Hey Cissy, how ya holdin' up?"

She closed the top of the grill and turned to Bad Billy. "I've been through a lot in my life, Billy; this has been the toughest thing that I've ever had to deal with. I don't know what I would've done without Cyrista, Lucas, and Mr. Payne. Now ya'll are here and helping."

She hung her head down and Bad Billy moved closer and put his big arms around her and said, "We'll be here till the end, girl. Hey, if its any help, Rider broke your ex dummy's nose real good."

She started laughing and said, "Yeah, that's what Cyrista told me after Mr. Payne called. I hear you and the boys did your parts too. Thanks, Billy. Thanks for bein' here when I need ya."

She looked up at Billy and he could see the pain in her eyes. He was a big bad ass, but Billy had a soft side to him also. He pulled her close to him and gave her a big, long hug.

"I needed that," she said as she hugged him back. "Give me one of those beers, Billy," she said as she broke their embrace. "I could use one. Hell, I could use two or three."

Cyrista came out with a large tray of buns and fixings for the burgers. She set it down and told the boys to help themselves. Then she disappeared back into the kitchen to fetch the potato salad and baked beans.

Everyone ate, drank, and had a good time telling stories about the fight that had taken place up at the shack. Gus had Cissy and Cyrista in stitches the way he relayed the story. He had a knack for making any story funny. Jimmy Legs and Bad Billy were still eating long after everyone else was done. Cyrista had to go back to the kitchen for more burgers to put on the grill.

CHAPTER SIX

It wasn't late, but things were winding down. Another long day had taken its toll on everyone. The Ancient One had just announced that he was ready to hit the hay when the phone rang. Cyrista went in to answer it and was back only a minute later. "That was Mr. Lee," she said. "He needs help pulling a roll away bed out of storage and taking it to room twelve."

The Ancient One got up to go, but Lucas volunteered. Cissy said that she would go and help. She knew Mr. Lee when he used to cook at the café and she hadn't seen him in a long time.

"Thank You, Lucas," Cissy started. "I owe you and Cyrista my life an' here ya are again today, sticking your necks out for me."

"You're welcome, Cissy," Lucas replied. "I did the only decent thing a man could do. I have my own score to settle with that bunch myself. I don't know if Cyrista told you, but they tried to do me in last week. That's how I got involved in this mess to begin with."

"Not to change the subject, Lucas, but I haven't

seen Cyrista this happy in a very long time. Y'all seem to be perfect for each other. I've known Cyrista since we were little girls, so take my word on it."

When they came around the corner of the motel they could see Mr. Lee in the office. He looked like he was reading something. As they drew closer, he looked up. Cissy smiled and waved to him. The light was off where the old vending machines were and the little hallway was dark. Lucas wasn't sure if there was even a light in there, so he didn't give it a second thought. When he put his hand on the doorknob he heard a noise behind him. Someone had come out of the darkness and grabbed Cissy.

As he turned to help, a crashing blow came out of nowhere It caught him on the left side of his head and brought him down on his hands and knees. All he could see was a white flash. He tried to shake it off but there was no time.

He heard someone's voice and felt the air forced out of him as a hard kick caught him in the ribs. The blow had lifted him off the ground and he landed on his side gasping for air. He looked up with blurred vision but could still make out who was giving him all this grief. His nose had two strips of tape across it and he was holding Cissy by the back of her hair. She was bent backwards and Lucas could tell that she was in pain. The big man had a mean look on his face, "How'd ya like that, Mr. Harley Rider." Lucas was trying to get to his feet when another hard kick to the same part of his head and this one took him down and out.

When Lucas came to, Cyrista was holding his head and gently wiping the injured side with a cold, wet towel. Slowly Lucas was regaining his senses. The voices he could hear sounded like they were a long ways off and he had foggy vision.

He tried to get to his feet when he heard Cyrista's angelic voice. "Hold on just a little bit, Lucas. We'll help you up.

"Gus, Billy, give me a hand here; he wants to get up."

Gus and Billy each got under an arm and slowly pulled Lucas up and then held him steady while he got his balance back. Billy kept a loose hand on him to make sure that he didn't go back down.

"Thanks, Billy," Lucas said. "The bastards got Cissy, didn't they?"

"They got her, all right, but not for long."

Lucas could hear the anger in Billy's voice and his own temper was beginning to boil.

Lucas was still a little wobbly when the Ancient One came over to him. Billy was holding on to him for a little assurance.

"Rider, I'm sorry about this, you seem to be getting the rough end of this shit." Lucas blinked his eyes a few times to focus on the old man. "I'm all right, Pap-Paw." He leaned back a little too far, but Bad Billy had him.

The Ancient One was in charge now, he was snapping out orders like a general on a battlefield. "Gus, Billy, get Rider up to the house. Cyrista needs to take care of him."

They also knew who was in charge and had Lucas up and gone in a matter of seconds. On the way up the steps, Billy asked Lucas if it was Cissy's ex. Lucas told him that it was and Billy began to cuss him.

Cyrista had an ice pack on Lucas's head as soon as Gus and Bad Billy had him in the chair. Lucas felt the side of his head and found two good-sized lumps as well as a couple cuts. The ice pack felt good. Cyrista held it on for a minute or two and then took it off. The swelling was under control, but Lucas's wound was an ugly black and blue.

The Ancient one came through the door. "Well, boys," he said, "I need to thank you. Looks like they've got the trump card again. Rider and I need to put together a plan. It's getting late and you boys have a long ride ahead of you."

Bad Billy jumped to his feet. "What?!" he shouted. "No way, Mr. Payne, not a chance! Those bastards come in here and trespassed onto my friend's property kidnap my girl and hurt my friend. No way, man, it don't happen that way with us. Play time is over, pay time is here."

Gus and Jimmy Legs had moved over and were standing next to Bad Billy. "Like he says, Mr. Payne, it won't happen that way with us," Gus said.

"Rider…" the old man got no response. "Rider," he said a little louder.

Lucas was almost out of it. He rolled his eyes in the direction of the Ancient One, "Yeah," he said in a nearly inaudible voice.

"You hold on, son. I've called Doc Pickett and he's on his way." The old man motioned for the boys to head out to the porch.

"Yeah, okay, Pap-Paw. I just need to rest for a minute. I'll be ready when you are."

The Ancient One had a look of true concern when he turned to Cyrista. "Baby girl, you take good care of my boy there."

A big lump came to Cyrista's throat when she tried to answer She had never heard Pap-Paw refer to anybody other than her daddy as his boy. "I'll take extra good care of him, Pap-Paw; don't you worry."

Everyone's emotions were running high in the old cabin, except for Lucas's. He did get a little choked up when Pap-Paw referred to him as "my boy", but he knew that the Ancient One and the boys wouldn't let him go with them to the old Stanley Place so he put on a good act for them. He knew that Cyrista knew how to get there and that he could convince her to tell him. He hated to be tricky and deceitful, but he had no choice in the matter.

He had certainly felt better in his life, but he had always had a way of making a quick comeback. He told Cyrista to get him some aspirin as he headed to the couch so he could lie down and concentrate. It was more a form of meditation to will himself past the pain and into a sense of well-being.

When Cyrista came out of the bathroom she saw Lucas lying on the couch and decided not to bother him. She tiptoed out to the porch but Pap-Paw and the boys had already gone down to the bikes.

Lucas's meditation was broken when he heard the bikes start up. He jumped to his feet and yelled "Cyrista!" She shot through the door, thinking something was wrong. To her surprise, he was standing in front of the couch smiling at her.

"Baby," he said, "You're going to have to trust me on this one. Pap-Paw and the boys' lives may depend on it."

"Are you okay, Lucas?" She looked like a little girl, too shy to say anything else.

"Yes, I'm fine. There's no time to explain right now. Trust me, please."

As he put on the bomber jacket that Pap-Paw had given him he told Cyrista to go get two pistols and the key to the truck. She didn't hesitate, shooting into Pap-Paw's room and then meeting Lucas out on the porch.

On the walk down to the truck he gave her the plan that he had come up with. He figured that Pap-Paw and the boys would do like they had earlier in the day and Lucas knew it wouldn't work as well a second time. The freaks would be ready and waiting for them. This time Lucas figured the timing would have to be perfect and take them by total surprise, and action would be the only way to handle it. He also knew that this would require a certain amount of luck.

Cyrista pulled out onto the road in the truck with Lucas following on his bike. The cool mountain air felt good to him. The further he rode, the more he was coming out of the trauma that the two licks to his head had put him through. Cyrista had come up with two pistols: one was her .45 and the other was an old Carl Walther 9mm. Her Daddy had taken the latter off of a German officer during the war. Lucas took the 9mm because he had one just like it, and he wanted Cyrista to have the .45 because she was familiar with it.

Cyrista flashed her lights and Lucas pulled up next to the driver's window. They slowed to about thirty miles per hours and Cyrista leaned out the window. "It's about a mile down the road on the left; you can't miss it. There's an old Gulf sign hanging on this side of the property.

"Lucas Payne, you be careful. I love you."

Lucas gunned the Harley and passed her, giving her the thumbs up as he did, and he was off. Little did he know that Pap-Paw and the boys were sitting at a little pull-off just ahead making last minute adjustments to their plan.

Lucas hit fourth gear and was laying the old

F.X.R.T. down. One thing about the old tour bike, it had the highest road clearance of any Harley made. Most of the time it was a pain in the ass to Lucas, but right now he liked it. The rice rockets had a hard time keeping up with him on the turns.

Pap-Paw and the boys could hear Lucas coming around the corner. At first they weren't sure if it was him or not. He had the Harley wound tight, but still had three thousand left and one more gear. He came by where they were sitting without a clue. The Ancient One looked at the boys and said, "Holy shit! That crazy ass thinks we're already there!"

He had no more gotten the words out when Cyrista drove by. "Shit! Go, boys, go!"

Lucas saw the Gulf sign and started to brake. He pulled in on the clutch. He didn't want them to hear him and loose the element of surprise.

As he got closer to the building, the old Stanley place began to look like the place that the delectable duo had taken him that night not so long ago. The cars were parked on both sides of the building, but there was a path through the center leading to the door. Lucas could hear the music inside. He couldn't help but wonder if they had someone inside setting them up for later.

He didn't see Pap-Paw or the boys' bikes anywhere. All he could do was hope that he hadn't arrived too late.

The door was about thirty yards from where he

was sitting. Lucas was not one to wait to do anything, once he had set his mind to it. He revved the engine and dropped the clutch. The Harley spun out with a squeal and he was moving toward the door.

The front wheel hit the door and it flew open with great force. Two or three people were knocked to the floor and out of the Harley's path. Lucas came right down the center of the floor. It was crowded and he bumped and hit six or seven people before he went down. Lucas had accomplished two of his goals right off the bat: there was confusion and panic with the people inside.

He was lying under the bike but it didn't have him pinned. Before he got up he reached into his coat and found the 9 mm. When he got to his feet, the first person he saw was Cissy's ex. The big dummy was coming straight at him so Lucas didn't wait for anything. He slammed one into the chamber, flicked off the safety and took a shot. The charging bull yelled and went down, holding his leg and yipping like a dog.

Lucas saw his next objective no more than two feet from him. It was Terry, just getting to her feet. Lucas realized that he was in the middle of the dance floor. He jumped forward grabbing her by her long hair and slammed the 9mm to her head. Just then he thought for sure that he was dead. Boom…boom…boom; three shots went off.

Spinning around, still holding onto Terry, Lucas

saw Pap-Paw, Gus, Bad Billy, and Jimmy Legs standing in the doorway.

Bad Billy was the first to move forward. He grabbed the first person that he came to and yanked the guy's head back hard by pulling his hair. The guy fell to the floor as Billy put an eight-inch blade to his throat. "Where is she?" he yelled. "Tell me or I'll cut your fucking head off."

"He don't know nothin', you stupid bull." To Lucas's surprise, it was Terry talking to Bad Billy.

Billy was in a rage. He slammed the guy's head down and in one movement he reached around another guy and came up with Tess. He pulled her close to him, yanked her head back and started to count as he brought the blade up to her neck. "One… two…three."

"No, don't!" Terry yelled. "She's in the back."

Bad Billy was headed toward the back. People were stepping on each other to get out of his way. Lucas looked over to Pap-Paw and the boys and said, "It's good to see you."

Gus and Jimmy Legs had somehow gotten a couple beers. They smiled and raised them to Lucas. Pap-Paw smiled and said, "Likewise, you crazy ass."

"Gus, Jimmy, would you do me a favor and get my bike out of here? I've kind of got my hands full right now."

"No problem, Rider," said Jimmy Legs. "I thought you did a real good job of parking it."

Gus and Jimmy Legs gave each other high five and laughed. By the time they had the bike outside, Bad Billy had come out with Cissy. She was wearing Billy's leather, but didn't look any worse for the wear they put her through.

"Rider, what's with the big dummy on the floor there?" The Ancient One was going to have a little fun with this since they had turned the tables and gotten the upper hand.

"Ya know, that guy was really beginning to piss me off. He thinks since he's so big and ugly that he can run over everyone, so I shot him," said Lucas.

The old man was smiling when he said, "I'll bet that hurt."

"Why don't we ask him?" Lucas looked down at the big man. "Did it hurt much when I shot you?"

The big dummy looked up at Lucas and snarled. The Ancient One was going to take this one to the limit. He turned to Lucas and said, "I don't like his attitude very much, Let's see if we can give him an adjustment."

The old man turned the .45 on the man who started squirming and begging. "Please don't shoot me again. Please, please, I'm begging you; don't shoot me, please."

"Well now, that's a little better," the old man said with a laugh. "Rider, I think he's beginning to nice'n up a little bit."

Bad Billy was standing behind the big man

holding on to Cissy. Without warning, he let go with a powerful kick to the back of his head. It was hard enough that it flipped the big man over and the front of his head hit the floor. He was out. Bad Billy stood there looking at the big man for a second, then at the Ancient One. In a very childlike manner he said, "Gee, I feel better about the whole thing."

The old man and Lucas burst out laughing. Lucas said, "Now I know how you got the name Bad Billy."

Of the fifty to sixty people in the building, not one of them was saying a word or moving a muscle. The Ancient One raised the .45 up over his head and let one go. "Everyone on the floor, and I mean now!"

The people were scared. They were dropping to the floor hard and fast. It had already been established that these riders were no joke. "Now that I have y'alls attention, I have something to say. Listen up! We're going to take your queen here with us. If one of you so much as farts, Rider here will blow her head off. Do you understand what I'm saying to far?" No one made a sound. The old man raised his voice and said, "Do you understand what I'm saying so far?!" This time he got replies from everyone on the floor. "That's better," he said. "Now we're going to go out that door and I don't want any one of you shit heads to move. When you can't hear these bikes anymore, then, and only then will it be safe to get up.

"Listen up. This is very important; I don't want any mistake about it. Tomorrow night, same time, same place, we'll bring this bitch back. I want that little girl here and she had better be unharmed or God help you, cause your devil wont be able to. That is not a threat, that's a promise."

The old man started backing out toward the door. He motioned for Lucas to follow him. He still had a good grip on Terry's hair and he pressed the 9mm harder to her head. Once they got outside, Lucas bent Terry over the back of the pickup that Cyrista was driving. "Jimmy Legs," he said, "get that rope laying up there and tie this bitch's hands behind her."

Jimmy Legs reached over and grabbed the rope. He started tying Terry's hands in back of her and she started to hiss and snarl at him. Bad Billy had just put Cissy in the front of the truck with Cyrista and they were hugging each other. Billy walked over to Terry and said, "If I hear one more sound out of that disgusting mouth of yours I'll cut your stinking tongue out." Terry became silent; she knew he meant what he said.

Lucas dropped that tailgate to the pickup and pushed Terry up into the back. He found a short length of rope and tied it around her neck and yanked it hard, pulling Terry to her knees. She looked up at Lucas and began to hiss at him. He took the other end of the rope and tied it off short to the back of the truck.

"There you go, bitch. You like treating people like dogs. See how you like being treated like one." He gave her a slight kick in the ass and her head banged against the side of the truck.

"You'll pay for this, you son-of-a-bitch," Terry hissed at him. "I swear to Diablo, you'll pay for this."

Lucas jumped on his bike. The other fellows had already mounted and cranked up and they were waiting on him. He yelled to Cyrista to go ahead, they would follow. Gus turned to Lucas and said, "I like your finishing touch up there. That'll give us something to watch on the ride back."

Lucas didn't realize what he had done until he looked up into the back of the truck and saw what Gus was talking about. When he pulled Terry down and tied her off to the truck her short miniskirt had gone up over her ass and it was staring them right in the face.

Lucas looked over at Gus and started to laugh. Gus gave him a high five and they all pulled out for the ride home. One thing no one could deny: Tess and Terry were both fine looking women with bodies to match. What a waste that they had to be stinking ass witches.

The ride back to the motel took about fifteen minutes. Once again, everyone was in high spirits and cutting up, even the Ancient One. When Cyrista got to the motel, she pulled up and backed along the front side of the building by the path leading to the cabin. She didn't want any of the customers to see what was going on. The guys all parked in front of the office where Mr. Lee could keep an eye on the bikes.

By the time the boys had parked their bikes and walked up along the path, Cyrista and Cissy had already gotten Tess out of the truck. She must have given Cissy a pretty rough time during her capture. It was out of character for Cissy; she had the short rope around Terry's neck and was pulling on it hard and cussing her. "If anything has happened to my baby, you don't have to worry about the men doing anything to ya. You'd better worry about me, you rotten, stinking, bitch."

No one interfered. They let Cissy yank, pull, and drag Terry up to the top of the stairs. If anyone had a right to punish Terry, it was Cissy.

When they reached the porch. Lucas took the rope from Cissy and tied it to the railing. Terry started in on him again. "Hey, bitch," he responded, "you had better cool down before I let this little wild cat loose on your ass, and I'll sit back and watch the show. It's up to you." Terry shut up and sat down on the floor of the porch.

The Ancient One called everyone to the far end of the porch. "It's early yet, but I want two people on guard up here all night. There's no telling what that bunch might do to get her back. We've got to keep her till we can make the exchange for the baby or all that we've done tonight was in vain." Everyone agrees.

Cissy said, "Thank you, once again. If it weren't for

y'all that bunch would be having their fun with me as we speak." She turned to Lucas and said, "God bless you, Lucas Payne. I thought for sure they'd killed ya." She put her arms around him and hugged him tight.

Lucas could feel a tear drip from her cheek. "It's all right, Cissy; I've got a think skull. It'll take a lot more than that to put me under." He held her tight and patted her on the back and reassured her that everything would work out.

"Look here, girl. If you don't know it by now I'll tell you: see that fellar right there? That's Bad Billy and he's pretty damn crazy about you. But I have to warn you about one thing: he's got a big, soft heart. Now, get over there, woman."

Cissy let loose of Lucas's neck and turned to Bad Billy. She threw her arms around his big neck and he bent over and picked her up with one arm. She planted a long, passionate kiss on him. Bad Billy gave Lucas the thumbs up with his free hand. Everyone laughed and cheered; they were beginning to think that things really would work out.

"Rider, are you trying to make me crazy?" the old man asked. "I almost had a stroke when you came tearing ass by us. Then there comes Cyrista bringing up your rear. I thought for sure that I'd have one.

"We no more than got off our bikes when I heard the shot. I thought for sure I'd walk in and find you dead. Boy, I'm too old for that shit; you got to learn to take it easy on the old man. Damn."

"Sorry, Pap-Paw," Lucas said. "I knew you wouldn't take me with me, so I went on my own. I was afraid you would approach it like we did up at the shack today, and I knew that wouldn't work twice in one day. The way I figured it, we had to get the drop on them and use the element of surprise. Hell, when I didn't see any bikes around, I thought they had your asses tied down inside. I couldn't let you boys have all the fun."

"Come here," the old man said. Lucas obeyed, not knowing what to expect. "You got more guts than you do sense, boy. How are ya feeling? Let me have a look at that head."

Lucas turned his head so that the old man could see it. The two knots were ugly; they had turned black and blue.

"Get your ass inside and let Cyrista put some ice on that. Hell, it hurts me to look at it. I'll be there as soon as we get the guard detail worked out." The Ancient One then slapped him on the back and handed him a beer out of the cooler.

Lucas walked by the boys, they slapped him on the back and added their two cents: "Yeah, like he said."

"Yeah, drink a beer. It couldn't hurt."

Bad Billy was the last to talk. "Yeah, Rider, thanks for what ya said a bit ago. Hey, you're one crazy little dude and I'm proud to have you as my friend. Lucas just shook his head and smiled back at all of them as he went into the house.

Lucas went inside, the Ancient One was smiling and shaking his head. He said to the boys, "I'm sure glad he's on our side."

"Yeah, me too," added Jimmy Legs. "He's got a big set. Hey, think about it: he went in there tonight thinking that we were down. He had no thought of not coming out of there or he wouldn't have left Cyrista waiting outside for him."

"Yeah," said Gus. "Once he gets his direction, get the hell out of the way."

"Well, boys," said the old man, "his name is Payne." He let out a big laugh.

"Lighten up, boys," he said. "Let's have a beer. We won tonight and we have the proof sitting right over there like a porch puppy."

Lucas woke up early. The sun was just beginning to break through the gray base of night. His head was lying on a pillow that was cradled by Cyrista who was sleeping soundly.

As slowly and quietly as he could, Lucas made his way to the kitchen. The front door leading to the porch was open. He stuck his head out and saw Gus and Jimmy Legs playing a game of cards. There must have been twenty beer bottles standing around them. Terry had her head resting against the railing of the porch. She didn't look like she had had a very good night. Her legs were tucked up under her and her miniskirt was riding high, exposing her little pink panties.

Sometime during the night, Gus and Jimmy Legs had switched from drinking beer to drinking coffee. Lucas was sure that the only reason for that was that the beer had run out. They both had pistols sitting on the arms of the old high back rockers.

They noticed Lucas at the same time. "Morning, Rider," they greeted him. "Old Doc Pickett came over right after you laid down. He said he'd look at you this mornin'. We played cards with him till he was broke." They both laughed at this and gave each other high fives. Gus was still laughing when Jimmy Legs continued. "Rider, this here is one cheatin' son-of-a-gun, but I'll be damned if I can catch him."

Gus looked at Lucas. "Damn, your head looks a whole lot better this morning."

Lucas hadn't even thought about it until now. He reached his hand up and felt it. It was sore, but he felt no swelling and the two little cuts had scabbed over. When he brought his hand down he noticed an oily substance on his fingers. Not thinking, he brought his hand to his face to smell. "Holy shit," he said as he jerked his head to one side. He had forgotten about the stuff that had been put on him the night that he first arrived there.

Gus and Jimmy Legs were both laughing at him. "Is that some foul smelling shit or what?" Gus said through his laughter.

"What the hell is it?" Lucas asked. "That's the

second time they used that shit on me."

"We don't know what the hell it is," answered Gus. "Cyrista and the old man are herbalists. They make all that stuff themselves. People come from all over to get shit from em. My mamma's been putting shit on me an givin' me stuff that they made since I was a little boy. It may not smell or taste very good, but I'm here to testify that it works."

Lucas went back into the kitchen. He washed his hands and got a cup of coffee. As he walked into the living room he heard a voice. It was old Doc Pickett on the sofa "Any more of that joe, Rider?"

"Yeah, sure, Doc. I'll get ya a cup."

"Black," the old Doc said as he unfolded from the sofa.

Daylight had broken and it looked like another perfect day in paradise. Lucas had just poured the old Doc's coffee when the Ancient One walked into the kitchen. "Thanks, Rider," he said, reaching for the cup of coffee. Doc walked in at the same instant and reached for the same cup of coffee. Doc was a little faster than old man.

"Thanks, Payne, you're a real gracious host." The two old men stood there exchanging glances at each other, then the old Doc took a sip of the coffee. "Not bad," he said.

"I'll get you another cup, Pap-Paw," said Lucas.

The Ancient One was mumbling under his breath. Lucas could tell that he was not much of a morning person either. He just needed a little space and a pot of coffee, same as Lucas.

The Ancient One walked out onto the porch. "Morning, boys. Any trouble last night?"

Gus looked up from the card game. "Morning, Mr. Payne. No, sir; all was quiet except for old Doc when we took his last dollar."

The old man chuckled and said, "Good for you, I mean, that's good. You boys had any sleep?"

Not breaking his view of the game, Jimmy Legs replied, "No, sir, but we're okay."

The old man looked down at the boys playing and said, "I hate to break up your fun, but I need you two fresh and on your toes tonight. I'll call down and ask Mr. Lee if anyone had checked out yet. You boys can get a few hours in down there. It looks like it's going to be busy up here today."

Jimmy Legs shook his head. "Whatever you say, boss."

The Ancient One walked back into the kitchen. Bad Billy and Cissy were sitting at the table drinking coffee. Cyrista was busy making another pot and Lucas had gone to the shower. This was all too much distraction for the Ancient One. He called out to the old Doc. "Doc, got your gear in the truck?"

"Yeah, Payne."

"Come on, lets you and me go fishing." The old Doc would rather fish than eat; he was ready.

The Ancient One walked in back of Cyrista. "Baby

girl, you're in charge. Get those two card-playing fools a room so they can get some sleep. Bring the girl in off the porch and feed her. Tell Rider to watch her while you and Cissy go down and do your chores; take Bad Billy with you. I don't want any surprises today. Me and my old buddy are going fishing."

She finished with the coffee and turned to give the old man a kiss. "You go and enjoy yourself; we have things under control here."

Lucas came out to find Bad Billy and Terry sitting at the Kitchen table eating breakfast. Cyrista and Cissy came out of her bedroom at the same time giggling like schoolgirls. Lucas suspected that they had been talking about him and Bad Billy. "Where's everyone else at?" Lucas asked.

"Well, that's a fine good morning," Cyrista said in a sarcastic tone.

"I'm sorry, baby. I've just got a lot on my mind with all this going on." He grabbed her by the hand and pulled her into the bedroom.

Putting his arms around her he said, "I'll show you a good morning if you have a little time."

She pulled him close and smiled as she felt him get excited. "I know things have been crazy here for the past few days, but it's soon to be all over. Then you had better watch out, buddy boy." She gave him a kiss.

"We've got to go down and do our chores at the motel. It shouldn't take too go long with the extra help I have."

They walked back to the kitchen still holding hands. Cyrista went to the coffee pot to pour Lucas a cup and started telling him what was going on. "Pap-Paw and Doc Pickett went fishing. Gus and Jimmy are getting a little sleep down at the motel. Pap-Paw wants Billy to go with me and Cissy while we change out the rooms. He wants you to stay here with Terry till we get back."

"Sounds like a plan to me. Get a move on; I already miss you." He swatted her on the butt as she turned to go. She turned back and gave him a kiss goodbye and went out the door with Cissy and Billy.

Lucas looked over to Terry. "Am I going to have to tie you back up or are you going to behave?" Something about her looked different to Lucas, but he didn't know what it was.

She smiled at Lucas and said, "I'll be a good little girl, Lucas. I'd like to take a shower if you would let me; I'm not used to sleeping out on the porch."

A light went off in Lucas's head: she was being too sweet. "I guess that'll be okay, but you'll have to leave the door open. I don't want you going out the window."

"Thank you," she said. "You can watch me if you want to."

To her surprise Lucas replied, "That's exactly what I'm going to do."

"Oh, good. I love it when a man watches me."

"Get moving before I change my mind."

He sat outside the bathroom door as Terry got undressed. Any man would have to admire a body such as she had. It was perfect. She slid out of her miniskirt with the grace of a dancer. Then she slowly pulled off her top, exposing her perfectly firm breasts and raising her arms high enough to give Lucas the full show. She stood there in her panties smiling at Lucas. "Why don't ya join me? That way you'll be sure that I won't escape."

It was hard for Lucas to say no. It would have been hard for any man to say no under the circumstances, but he was proud of himself when he said, "If you don't take your shower now then the only thing you're going to get is a kick in the ass."

"Ya can't blame a girl for tryin'. If you remember, Lucas Payne, I've had you and I know what's good; and baby, you're good."

"Thank you, Terry. Now get in the shower or get your clothes back on." Terry knew she was getting nowhere so she took her shower and got dressed.

Lucas took her into the living room after her shower and told her that she could lie on the couch if she wanted to get some sleep. "You couldn't have gotten much sleep last night out on the porch."

She gave him a puzzled look and said, "Why are you being so nice to me, Lucas, after all we've done to hurt you."

Lucas didn't have a quick answer, but after thinking for a minute he replied, "The answer is obvious, Terry. We all were put here to live and die. It's easy to die if you're at peace with yourself and the world; it doesn't matter how big or small your world is. All you have to do is live easy with it.

"I know the difference between right and wrong. It's taken me a long time to look and understand just how simple it can be. My answer to you is time and place. Last night, if anything had gone wrong, you wouldn't be here today to ask me that question. This is a different time and place. Right now, you are not my enemy unless you choose to be. I hope that after tonight this whole mess dries up and goes away, but I really don't think that will happen.

"It's easy for me. I take life as it comes to me and I deal accordingly. The same way with people: it all depends on how and what they come at me with that will determine how I treat them. Right now, you're acting like a real person, so I'll treat you like one. Tomorrow you might get in my cross hairs and I'll have to pull the trigger."

"Lucas," she said, "you're very lucky to have a woman like Cyrista in your life. I've always admired her from a distance. She's so strong and she's loyal to that old man; not to mention that she's the most beautiful woman that I've ever seen. She really seems to have her life in order and she's always cheerful and happy."

She sounded like she was being honest and

sincere in what she was saying, maybe even a little envious of Cyrista. Lucas wasn't going to take any chances with her; he had already seen what a good actress she was. "You need to get a little sleep while you can. They'll be back up here before long."

He knew that Terry wasn't through. She had a look of determination. "Lucas," she said, "there is a way to end this. I want you, Lucas. I can give you power, wealth, sex, anything you want. Now that I've seen what kinda man you are, I can see how beneficial you'd be with us, given a little guidance and direction. Together we'd be unstoppable."

For a moment, Lucas just stared at Terry. She wouldn't give up; nothing would stop her. "Terry, I've always admired a worthy foe, and you are just that. If you would have come to me three years ago you would own my soul right now. The things you're offering were the most important things in the world to me. But something happened to me while I was in prison: I rid myself of the evils that you hold so high. I've denounced Satan and taken Jesus Christ into my heart.

"You and yours may win this battle, but you will never win the war. Your direction is wrong, Terry, and you need to see that before it's too late. I'm no preacher. Hell, I'm not even a good Christian, but I know the difference between right and wrong. Your way is wrong. Id rather die for something right than live with something that is wrong."

"Those are strong words you speak, Lucas Payne. What a waste. You're marked, Lucas; you can never win. We are too many, and too strong. It will be a shame and a waste to kill you, but you will die."

It was extremely hard for Lucas to hold his temper, especially after what she had just said. But he stayed calm. "You are in no position right now to be giving me threats, my dear. All I have to say to you is get it done. Take me down. So far, all you and your idiots have managed to do is steal a helpless child, and, by God, that will end tonight. Now, shut up before I tie you up and treat you like the dog you are."

It was over. She had nothing more to say to him and he was through with her. She had gone too far and he had taken it well, but he was pissed. She rolled over on the couch, turning her back to him.

Lucas knew the odds were against them. He had been up against odds his entire life and was still standing. Maybe this time his luck would run out. He was well aware that he could go down, but Lucas had a side of him that could accept that. He knew that if he did go down, it wouldn't be without a fight. Being on the right side felt good to him. He knew that he didn't have any magical answers, but for some reason he had survived a lot of shit in his life. Maybe this was the reason why. If it was, then so be it. He could live or die with that.

Lucas sat in the silence of the morning. Nothing but the sounds of nature was around him. The windows were open and the warm, late summer's breeze and the peaceful sounds were all over him. He was in touch with his spiritual side. It didn't come to him often, but when it did he welcomed it. He felt the strength that the inner peace gave to him, and he prepared himself for what was to come.

Cyrista, Cissy, and Bad Billy came back to the cabin. It had taken Cyrista a little longer than she thought it would. Lucas hadn't realized how long he had been sitting there, deep in thought and enjoying his tranquil state until he walked into the kitchen and looked at the clock.

Cyrista was quick to pick up on the change or state that Lucas had just come out of. "Lucas, what's wrong with you? You seem different somehow."

"I'm fine, pretty baby. I've just been doing some thinking. You know, kind of a self evaluation." He walked up in back of her and gently put his arms around her and very softly kissed her on the back of the neck.

"Ahhh, I don't know what it is, but I like it," she said softly as she tilted her head back to expose more of her neck.

"Any trouble out of our charming house guest?" she asked.

"Nothing I couldn't handle. We had a little chat and I told her to shut up so she rolled over on the couch and has been sleeping ever since."

She turned around in his arms and laid her head

on his shoulder. He held her, gently rubbing her back up and down for a long time. "Hey," she said breaking the silence, "are you hungry? I'll fix us something to eat."

"Hey, yourself. How about you call in a couple of pizzas and me and Bad Billy will ride into town and get them. You have been going non-stop for days."

She smiled at him and said, "You got a deal."

Lucas grabbed the keys to the pickup and was headed out the door. He stopped in the doorway, turned to Cyrista and said, "If she wakes up just shoot her."

"Or better yet," Billy added, "turn Cissy loose on her."

Cyrista stood there shaking her head. "You two buttheads just go and get the pizzas. I'll order three for when Gus and Jimmy wake up."

Bad Billy turned to Lucas and said, "Oh, now we're buttheads. Come on butthead, let's go before we turn into something bigger and better."

They were laughing when Lucas said, "What would that be? Bikers?"

"Good one, Rider. Good one," Billy said, and they were gone.

Lucas looked over at Bad Billy as he pulled out of the motel. He could tell that he was up since they got Cissy back. "Things going well between you and Cissy, I trust?"

"Yeah, Rider, she's one hell of a gal.

"Ya know, Rider, a lot of people think that just because we're bikers we don't have the capacity to care about people and have a love life like anyone else. Sure, we're a little different. We enjoy the freedom that we take. Our priorities might be a little different too, but when it comes right down to it, we hurt, we care, and we have feelings and beliefs like anyone else."

"Ya know, Bad Billy," Lucas said, "you know that I know that, and that's what's important. To hell with those people that are so narrow-minded that they have to stereotype us to some movie they saw fifteen years ago. Look at what's going on right now. How many people would stand up against what has been happening around here for a lot of years? Those same people that you're talking about would rather turn their heads and look the other way. We're the righteous ones here. We don't close our eyes and hide behind locked doors. Hell, Billy, I'm not telling you anything you don't already know."

Bad Billy was thinking about what Lucas had just said, but his thoughts were broken when he looked into the rear-view mirror. "Get down, Rider!" he yelled. They both ducked at the instant the back window was blown out and glass flew everywhere.

Bad Billy looked back up to the road just in time to see the curve. He turned hard to the left and started to skid, but pulled it out in time to make the curve.

"Shit!" Lucas yelled. "Where in the hell did they come from?"

Just then another blast went off. This shot was low, hitting the tailgate of the truck. Lucas and Bad Billy were both looking for a gun but then realized that they had left without one. Lucas turned to look back and saw that the gun being used against them was a double barrel shotgun.

Their attackers had to reload. "Hit it, Billy! See if you can put a little distance between us."

"Done deal," Bad Billy replied.

Lucas looked into the back seat of the truck and saw there were six of the one by three boards with nails still in the back seat of the truck. "I've got something for em," Lucas yelled back to Bad Billy as he leaned out the broken back window.

Bad Billy made another sharp curve to the left. When he had gained the right distance between them, Lucas started throwing the nailed boards out and over the tailgate. He had tossed five of them out and he took the last one and threw it straight up into the air. The driver saw the airborne board and swerved hard to the left.

"Bingo," Lucas yelled. The truck hit two of the five boards with the driver's steering tire and back tire. The truck swerved back hard to the right, but it was too late; the damage was done. The tires were going down quick.

Bad Billy was looking in the rear view mirror

seeing the same thing Lucas was. The attack truck went to the left and the driver pulled it back hard to the right. The rims of the flat tires dug into the pavement and the truck flipped. The cab hit the road and the truck went airborne. It flipped one and a half times in the air before crashing back down to the pavement with great force. The truck exploded into flames as it went skidding down the road on its top with its parts flying everywhere. Bad Billy and Lucas both knew that nothing would live through a crash like that.

Bad Billy's eyes were as big as silver dollars and his mouth was hanging wide open. "Damn, Rider, I ain't never seen anything like that before. Shit fire, Rider they got to be dead."

Lucas was still in shock over the crash he had just caused and didn't know what to say. He looked over at Bad Billy and said, "This had better be some good pizza we're picking up."

Bad Billy burst out laughing. "You're one crazy dude, Rider."

They were at the edge of town when Lucas said, "Stop and get the pizza, Billy. I'll call the girls and tell them to be on their toes and not to worry; we'll be a little longer than we thought."

When Bad Billy got back into the truck with the pizzas he asked, "Well, Rider, how'd it go?"

"I told them we saw a wreck on the way into town and it would take them a while to clean it up. Let's go down to Sam's and have a cold beer. We've got a little time to kill.

Bad Billy was laughing, "You've got a way with words, Rider."

They pulled up in front of the bar. It was early, but there were five trucks sitting out front. Bad Billy looked hard at one of them and said, "Isn't that old Doc Pickett's truck, Rider?"

Lucas looked but wasn't sure if it was. He had been worried about those two old birds ever since Cyrista told him they had gone fishing early that morning. He was hoping it was them.

The door to the bar was open; Lucas let Billy walk in first. It was a habit to let whomever he was with go first.

"Hey boys." Lucas was glad to see the old Doc and the Ancient One sitting at the bar. They were listening to Sammy's police scanner. "Fishing…you two look like you're fishing."

The two men looked at each other. The Ancient One spoke first, "Go out there and look in the coolers. We hit a honey hole that you wouldn't believe. Hell, we caught a little bit of everything: trout, bass, we even caught a few big ol' catfish. We wore em out for a while."

Sammy set a beer in front of each of them and said, "Did ya boys hear bout the bad wreck up on the highway?"

Lucas and Bad Billy looked at each other. The

Ancient One picked up on it. Sammy went on, "Yeah, two ol' boys were dead. They had to call the fire department out. Seems the truck caught fire an' everything."

Lucas looked over at the Ancient One and said, "Let's go take a look at those fish."

The old man had a worried look on his face as they walked outside. Once out the door he said, "Rider, what's up?" Lucas walked to the backside of the pickup. Without saying a word he pointed to the back window and the tailgate.

"Holy shit, you boys all right?" the Ancient One asked.

"Yeah, we're okay, but the ass holes that did this aren't. They're laying up on the highway being cooked in that pickup truck."

The Ancient One looked down at the ground and shook his head. "What happened, Rider?"

Lucas ran the story down to the old man in detail. The old man looked at where the back window had been, then at the tailgate. He put his hand on Lucas's shoulder. "This whole deal is about to come to a head, Rider. We've been giving them bastards hell and now you and Bad Billy have gone and taken out two more of them. Tonight is going to be very dangerous, Rider. They will want to pay us back for all the grief we've been giving them…Come on, let's get our asses home."

The last of the clean up was being done by the

time Bad Billy and Lucas made it to the site of the accident. The truck was sitting on the back of the pull up wrecker on the side of the road. There sure wasn't much left of it though. The cab was smashed even with the hood and the rear was nearly cut in two; not to mention it was burned to a crisp.

Lucas and Bad Billy were both quiet. Neither of them liked the fact that two people had died, even if they had been trying to kill them. Lucas looked up to Bad Billy and said, "This thing has gotten ugly, Billy.

"The old man is right: tonight is going to be bad. Those suckers are going to want to pay us back. We've got to have our shit together if we want to see daylight tomorrow."

Chapter Seven

The rest of the drive back to the cabin was in silence. By the time Lucas and Bad Billy had returned, the Ancient One and Doc were already there. Lucas took the pizza up to the cabin while Billy went to see if Gus and Jimmy Legs were still sleeping.

When Lucas reached the porch he knew there had been trouble. The screen door was hanging by one hinge and had been ripped and broken out in the center. Lucas's heart dropped as he entered the kitchen, the table was knocked over and the floor was littered with things that had been sitting on it.

"Pap-Paw!" he yelled.

"Back here, Rider."

Lucas walked back to the old man's bedroom. Doc and the Ancient One were just standing there looking around. The room had been taken apart pretty good. Whoever had done this was definitely looking for something. The back door leading to a small deck was standing wide open. Lucas could smell the wild flowers that grew on the side of the mountain behind as a slight breeze blew through the window.

"Well, Rider," the old man said in a very low voice, "this puts a new light on the whole situation. In all the years I've been doing battle with these low-lives they've never gone this far."

The old man turned to look at Lucas. It almost scared him when he looked into the old man's eyes. He had been in a lot of situations and seen men that had been broken, hurt, and angered to the point of killing, but nothing had ever prepared him for what he saw in the eyes of the Ancient One. His eyes were on fire; he had transformed from a mild, loving old man into a demon.

No one spoke for the next few minutes, and the short time seemed to lapse into hours. Finally the Ancient One said, "They have gone too far this time. They have taken the last and only thing I live for." His voice dropped low and his words came out slowly. "I guess I've always known it would come down to this final battle that only one can walk away from."

He stopped for a second and looked into Lucas's eyes. Lucas felt as if his soul had been exposed for the whole world to see as the old man looked at him. Before he could talk, Lucas moved closer to him and put his hand on the old man's shoulder. "Yes, sir, Pap-Paw. If its death they want, then so be it." Nothing else had to be said. Lucas and the Ancient One were connected; bound like twins at birth.

When Lucas looked around he noticed that the old Doc was gone. He hadn't seen him leave and it made him wonder how long the Ancient One had been standing there.

When they walked out to the kitchen, Doc and Billy had already fixed the screen door. Even though people were in the house, it seemed empty. Lucas looked around and felt the loneliness. He and Cyrista hadn't been together very long, but the connection was there. She had brought feelings back to life that he had thought were dead for a long time. The only word he knew for it was love.

Lucas knew he would have to prepare himself and be ready for combat, but this was like no other combat he had been involved in. In the past, it was himself. He had never had so much at stake. A hollow feeling was coming over him. He didn't mind dying himself, but Cyrista and the Ancient One were a different story. The "what if's" of the situation were beating the hell out of him. He knew he had better get his shit together and do it quickly.

"Rider, I'll be down at the shed for the rest of the afternoon. Come on down when you get ready to talk and we'll plan for tonight." The Ancient One knew he needed time alone to prepare himself. They didn't have to speak of feelings, it was understood. Together they could act and react from one another without saying a word.

The Ancient One grabbed a couple slices of pizza

and headed for the shed. The old Doc and Bad Billy were busy picking up the mess the kidnappers had left. Lucas didn't feel like talking to anyone. He needed to be alone and the others sensed it.

Not knowing where he was going, he too grabbed a couple slices of pizza and headed out the door. Eating as he walked, he found himself standing in front of the gate to the family cemetery. He opened it and walked to the homemade bench, sat down, and lowered his head.

He sat for some time before he lifted his head to look at the tombstone bearing his name. "I didn't know you when you were alive, but I feel like I know you real good. Thanks for your time and advice; we'll talk again real soon."

He got up and looked around to make sure nobody was watching him. It wasn't that he felt stupid talking to the grave of a man he'd never met, it was private, though, and he wanted to keep it that way.

Walking toward the shed, Lucas felt as though the world had been lifted from his shoulders. He had a calm, easy feeling about himself and was prepared for whatever the night ahead might bring him.

He walked into the shed the old man greeted him as if nothing in the world was wrong. "Hey, Rider, do you feel better?"

Lucas smiled at the Ancient One. "Yeah, I feel much better. How about you?"

"Yeah, I'm at peace with what has to be done. Like

you, I just needed a little time to get my shit together."

They both laughed and the old man handed Lucas a jug. "Go easy, boy. That shine is older than you are."

Lucas grabbed the jug and turned it up. He took a good pull out of it before setting it down. To his surprise, it was smoother than any whiskey he'd ever had. The Ancient One was smiling and waiting for his reaction. "Damn," Lucas said, "that's the best I've ever had, bar none."

The Ancient One laughed. "That's what everybody says. My brothers made the best shine that a man could put to his lips. That's why they did so good when they were in business."

Still smiling he said, "Follow me, Rider." He walked to the back of the shed. Lucas followed him down the heavy, hand made stairs and was totally surprised when they reached the bottom. It wasn't dug out, as he would have expected it to be. It was a cave.

Lucas's mouth was hanging open as he looked at all the jugs of whiskey. They were stacked on shelves from the floor to the ceiling of the cave. There must have been five hundred or more of the old, clay jugs. "Holy shit," he said as he viewed the cave.

The Ancient One chuckled and said, "I didn't know what to do with it, so I put it here for safe keeping. It's been here a long time and keeps getting better with age."

Lucas saw that there were five or six old wooden crates sitting around as well as a multitude of home canned vegetables of all kind.

"Rider, grab that bag over there and bring it up with ya. But be careful with it."

He grabbed the bag and followed the old man up the stairs with it. "What's in it?" he asked.

The Ancient One took that bag and told Lucas to close the trap door. "Oh, I've got a little of this and that in there. But mostly, it's what's going to give us our edge tonight."

The old man rolled a big trunk and tire rack over the trap door. When he was finished, there was no sign of the door being there. Lucas smiled at him and said, "A person could go down there and sit out World War III and not care when it was over."

The old man just smiled at Lucas, he took the bag, and headed for the door. When he had locked it he put his hand on Lucas's shoulder. "Rider, I'm glad that you're here. I think you were sent to us to put an end to this evil here in my valley.

"Go up to the cabin. I've got to stop at those two card playing fools rooms and get them to take care of something for us. Then I'll see Mr. Lee and be right up. We'll talk about our plan then."

Lucas felt good that the Ancient One wanted him there. He had grown to love the old man in the short time they had been together. He also had mixed feelings about his role in the situation that was at hand. If he hadn't gone this way and hadn't stopped here to lick his wounds and if he and Cyrista hadn't fallen in love... if only he would have listened to his better judgment none of this would have happened.

He stopped at the front porch and looked out over the valley below. He loved it here and felt like he had finally found a place where he belonged. His thoughts went to Cyrista; he was worried about her. Then he became angered that they could take the only thing from him that mattered. After he said a silent prayer for Cyrista's safety, he asked for the strength and courage to do whatever he had to do, and to live through it.

He was headed into the cabin when he heard the pickup truck leaving and the Ancient One coming over the footbridge. He waited for the old man to go inside.

"Hey, Rider," the old man said as he was half way up the steps, "any of that pizza left?"

Lucas waited for him to reach the top step before he answered. "I don't think even Bad Billy and Doc could finish off three extra large pizzas by themselves.

"Where'd you send Gus and Jimmy off to?"

The old man gave Lucas a sly smile and said, "We'll all talk when they get back. Ain't no need till then."

Lucas took the Ancient One for his word and didn't ask any more questions. He knew by the look the old man had given him that he was up to something. They went inside and started on the pizza and beer.

They were all sitting out on the porch when they saw the pickup return. Gus and Jimmy Legs came running around the corner of the motel and didn't stop until they got to the top of the stairs. Both were grinning from ear to ear, but were to out of breath to say anything. Gus lifted his head, still breathing hard, and gave the Ancient One thumbs up.

"I've still got the touch," Gus said. "You should have seen it…it was perfect." He was as excited as a kid who had just ridden his bike for the first time.

He started to go on but the old man stopped him. "Hold on, Gus. I haven't told them what's going on yet."

"What the hell is going on?" Lucas asked with a half smile on his face.

"Well, Gus here used to handle explosives for the state highway department," the Ancient One started, "so I sent him and Jimmy Legs up to the old Green place to blow it up.

"That was dynamite in that bag you carried up for me, Rider. That way I see it, tonight will be tough enough, and if they got us inside then they'd have the edge. I thought it would give us the edge to have our little meeting outside so we all could be placed where it will do us the most good."

"You sly old dog," Lucas said as his half smile grew into a broad one.

"I wouldn't be smiling too big, Rider. You are the one who's going to be in the center of the action.

You're the one they want, but if everyone does his job tonight and they don't have too many surprises for us, we might just get the girls back and live to talk about it."

The Ancient One was looking Lucas right in the eyes. He sure knew how to put a damper on the mood. But Lucas had already figured he would be the center of things tonight and he was prepared for it... in his mind anyway. Now he wanted to hear the rest on the Ancient One's plan. He thought he should have the last say-so on it, since it was putting his ass on the line.

For the next three hours they went over the plan, time and time again. Lucas suggested only a few, small changes, but overall everyone was comfortable with it. It was well thought out. Now was the hard part: the wait. Lucas had always hated that part.

Everybody was cheerful and joking, trying to take the nervous edge off. Gus and Jimmy Legs made a beer run, but came back with only a twelve pack. They would be the first to leave to get in place before the evil bunch got there. Lucas tried to take a nap, but he had too much on his mind. Old Doc and the Ancient One went down to the truck to get the fish they had caught earlier in the day. They cleaned them and went into the kitchen to cook up a good meal before the time came to go.

Shortly before sundown, Doc loaded up Gus and Jimmy Legs along with two high-powered rifles and a bag of goodies. Lucas found out that Gus not only handled the explosives for the state, but was also U.D.T: underwater demolitions team when he was in the Navy. He knew his shit when it came to blowing things up. U.D.T. was the next thing to Nave Seal and Lucas had a high regard for anyone that was or had been a Seal.

He had learned a lot about all the guys while they sat around killing time that afternoon. He felt a lot better about going into the lion's den after learning of the experience he had backing him up.

Jimmy Legs had been with the twenty-fifth infantry in Vietnam. The 25th had more time in field than any outfit that had fought there. Jimmy Legs didn't say too much about it, but he didn't have to. Lucas knew he had seen plenty of shit if he was in the 25th.

Bad Billy had served with the fifth Special Forces and still would be if he hadn't broken some smart ass, know it all, chocolate bar's jaw. Billy had chosen to make a career of the service, and he had eight years in when his little mishap took place. He had no choice, they asked him to resign of face court martial charges and possible dishonorable discharge. He talked to Lucas the most out of all the guys; they had a lot in common.

While Lucas and Bad Billy had been talking, they learned that they knew some of the same people. Lucas was an ex-Airborne Ranger and had been assigned once to a C.I. team for his last nine months of service. One had to like living on the edge, having your ass in the wind for that sort of thing. No matter how much experience one had on the edge, one couldn't help but have a case of the jitters when about to face the unknown.

The Ancient One had filled them in on everything that he knew about the bunch of heathens that they were up against. Everyone knew what they had to do and felt good about his part. Lucas knew he was going to be the bait. He would have no cover and nowhere to hide. He would be the main attraction; everyone else would watch and follow his lead. If anything were to go wrong, he knew he would be the first to go down, but he had made his peace and was ready to face it.

It was time.

Chapter Eight

When it was time to leave the cabin the Ancient One called Lucas into his bedroom. "Rider, we haven't known one another for long, but it has been quality time that we have spent together. You're so much like my son was; I feel close to you. I feel as if my son lives through you. It's given me a lot of pleasure and I don't want it to end. Good luck, son, and be careful. I want you to have this." The Ancient One gave Lucas a hug and walked out of the room.

Shortly after the Ancient One, Lucas came out of the room. He was wearing the bombers jacket and had the 9mm stuck in the back of his belt. "Let's rock and roll." Bad Billy gave him a high five and the four of them were out the door. Lucas and Billy led the way to their Harleys. Old Doc and the Ancient One followed them in Doc's pickup truck. They rode slowly, enjoying the cool air of the late summer's evening.

They pulled off the road and drove up to what used to be the old Green place. Lucas had to smile when he saw what Gus had done.

The old building was lying in a neat pile. It was as if someone had folded all of its sides into the center. The old chimney was still intact except for a few missing bricks. There was very little debris scattered around. One look at it and Lucas knew that Gus was no doubt an expert.

To the right side of where the building was, there was a clearing and a small hill. Lucas could see seven people standing in the center of it and about ten to the left. Lucas and Bad Billy parked and climbed off their bikes as Pap-Paw and Doc pulled up behind them. Lucas started his lonely walk toward the little hill as Bad Billy met old Doc and the Ancient One in front of the pickup truck.

Lucas stopped about twenty feet in front of the center group of people on the hill. Cyrista, Cissy and the little girl were standing together with two big goons behind them. Terry stood to their right and Tess to their left. The three girls had their hands behind their backs, so Lucas figured they were tied.

Lucas kicked it off, "Let the girls go and we won't have any trouble. I've come to make the exchange: me for the girls. You have my word that I won't lift a finger if you let them go."

Terry moved around in front of her captives. She pointed her finger at Lucas and said, "You are a fool, Lucas Payne, and you will die tonight."

Lucas didn't hesitate to answer even though he

knew she wasn't finished speaking. He just wanted to see how fast he could piss her off. "I came here tonight to die, bitch, but you're going to take the trip with me. I'll send you to hell where you belong." He smiled at her and put his hands to his hips to mock her.

Everyone was waiting for Terry to respond. Bad Billy was smiling and nudged the Ancient One in the ribs. "He's not bluffing," the old man said as he leaned over to Bad Billy.

His plan was working; he could see the anger building in her. "What are you doing, bringing all these people with you, Lucas Payne? We said it would be you and the old one there. You can't even follow simple rules."

Lucas knew the drill: it was her turn to try to piss him off. He would have nothing to do with it. "You and your bunch of heathens threw the rule book out the window when you trespassed onto the cabin today."

He had reversed it once again; she was getting pissed. Her voice went up a pitch or two as she started in on Lucas. "You've got a lot of nerve, Lucas Payne. You and your big dummy killed two of my high priests today and you stand there telling me about rules."

This toying back and forth was not Lucas's style. He would get her this time for sure. "Well now, its not my fault your so called "high priests" are too dumb to read a driver's manual."

Terry's hand shot up in the air and pointed straight at Lucas. Out of nowhere came a flash of light, like a small bolt of lightning and it hit Lucas right in the middle of his chest. His feet came straight up into the air and he flew backwards five or six feet.

Cyrista screamed, "Lucas!" and tried to move to him, but the goon behind her grabbed hold of her. Bad Billy also lunged toward him, but the Ancient One got hold of his wrist.

Terry was about to say something. She thought she had everything under her control; then she heard Lucas laughing. Her mouth dropped open as she stared at him. He got to his feet, brushing off the dust as he did so. His shirt was still smoking as he brushed at it with the back of his hand.

Cyrista had come from tears to laughter, Cissy and her little girl stood there in amazement. Old Doc and Bad Billy looked on in shock and the Ancient One just chuckled and shook his head.

Lucas was still brushing at his shirt when he looked up at Terry. He had a big smile on his face and he could see the anger and dismay on hers. "That's a very nasty habit: smoking people." He laughed and said, "Is that the best you can do? Is that all you have? And you call yourself a witch."

She was visibly shaken by this time and Lucas knew what was coming next; he readied himself. Terry raised her hand to the back of her head like she was getting ready to throw a ball. She spoke some of the mumble jumbo stuff and let it fly. Lucas was concentrating on what he had learned in baseball when he was a kid: Never take your eye off the ball. Follow it from when it leaves the pitcher's hand.

This one was easy. She was upset and let loose with a wild one. He saw that it was going to fall short. He stood there as cool as he could be under the circumstances. He crossed his arms and legs to appear relaxed and waited for it to hit. It hit a little closer to him than he thought it would, but he didn't mind; it made for a better show. He felt a small shock to his left leg and dirt flew up over his head. That one had been bigger and more powerful than the first.

He uncrossed his legs and stood with his hands in the direction of the people to the left and right. "This is what you all follow: a witch that can throw electric spit balls? Get a life!" Then he laughed. He could hear a low roar of the people talking as he looked into the angry eyes of Terry. He could tell that the last one she let go had taken a little wind out of her.

A few of the people from each side of the hill were moving in the direction of their parked cars. "Stop! Stay where you are. This ain't over yet"

Tess moved up by her side but Terry pushed her away. More people began moving toward their cars. Terry was so upset that she began to shake. She let go with another bolt, this time not at Lucas, but at the group of people headed toward the cars. It was a warning shot over the heads of the people and into the trees behind them.

Lucas looked at the people and was shaking his head. "Ya see? She'll stop at nothing to get her way. She'll turn on you or anyone else in her own self-interest. Go on, get out of here; this is between me and this pitiful thing."

"Lucas Payne!" she screamed, "You will die for this!" She let go with three bolts. The first hit to the left, so Lucas jumped to the right. The next hit to the right and Lucas jumped to the left. The third was low and would have hit him below the knees, but Lucas jumped up and it hit the ground.

"Yee Haw!" Lucas cheered. He was having fun with this. Laughing and doing a little dance he looked over to his friends standing in front of the truck and they were laughing just as hard as he was. He gave them thumbs up and they gave him one back.

Terry had fallen down on her knees and was bent over with her hands in front of her holding her up. Tess was standing next to her and had drawn her arm back as if she was going to throw another bolt at Lucas. The Ancient One saw this and pulled his .45 from his belt. He fired a shot into the air to get her attention and said, "I wouldn't do that if I were you."

Tess was dropping her hand slowly when she turned to the goons standing behind the girls and yelled, "Kill them! Kill them!"

The one to Lucas's right didn't move, but the one on the left who was closest to Cyrista raised a three-foot machete above his head. Lucas pulled the 9mm from behind his back but couldn't get a clear shot. The Ancient One aimed but he too was blocked by Cissy's head and couldn't get a clear shot.

Cyrista didn't know what was going on until she heard the shot ring out and the goon yipped like a dog. She turned in time to see the machete falling from his hand and the machete hitting him in the leg.

Jimmy Legs stood up about fifty yards away and lifted his rifle up over his head. Lucas lifted his 9mm over his head and waved back to Jimmy Legs. "Way to go, Jimmy. Great shot," Lucas yelled to him.

All but a few of the people who were at the hill had gone to their cars and were making an exit. One of the two goons yelled, "Hey, just let us get out of here. We don't want any more trouble."

Lucas motioned with the gun in his hand to go ahead and they didn't waste any time. The goons were running for the last pickup parked there.

Cyrista came running from the hill toward Lucas. Her hands were still tied behind her back. Lucas opened his arms and she fell into them. Bad Billy and Cissy were moving toward each other with Cissy's little girl following close behind. Gus and Jimmy Legs began making their way to join everyone else.

The old Doc had an arm around the Ancient One's shoulders and said, "Well, Payne, it's finally all over."

"Not yet, Doc."

Just then, Tess let out a blood-curdling scream that could pierce an eardrum. Everyone stopped and looked at her. They could all hear the noise, but no one knew what it was. It was coming from the woods behind where the building had been. The brush was rustling and a low growling sound was moving toward them.

Lucas pulled Cyrista behind him; they were closest to the sound. Jimmy Legs and Gus stopped walking and pulled their rifles into a ready position. Old Doc and the Ancient One moved to the side of the pickup and also pulled out their guns to the ready mark. Bad Billy had reached Cissy and the little girl and had them standing behind him. He was ready.

Out into the clearing came a pack of wild dogs. They were running at a high speed straight toward Lucas and Cyrista. Foam dripped from their mouths as they showed their teeth. Lucas, being the closest let the first shot rip. The lead dog dropped and rolled. All hell broke loose: everyone was firing and the wild dogs were dropping, but there must have been at least twenty of them.

Lucas had emptied his 9mm while there were still more dogs coming and the pack was getting closer. All he could do was stand in front of Cyrista and pray that the other guys didn't miss. A few of the dogs had stumbled over ones that had been shot; they were getting to their feet and resuming their charge.

Shots rang out from everywhere, and then became silent all at once. All of the dogs were down except for two that had just gotten back to their feet. A shot sounded out; Lucas could tell it was a rifle. One of the last two dogs fell. The remaining dog wasn't more than six feet from Lucas. He dropped the 9mm and pulled out the k-bar. The wild dog jumped straight at Lucas's face. He never heard that shot that Jimmy Legs squeezed off just in time.

The big dog hit Lucas square in the chest. They went down, knocking Cyrista off her feet as they did. He had a hold of the dog and rolled over on top of it with the k-bar drawn back to make what he thought would be the fatal blow. He looked down at the wild dog and realized that it was already dead. Jimmy Legs had landed one right between its eyes as it made its final leap at Lucas. He rolled over onto his back and let out a sigh of relief. "Thank you, Lord," he said out loud.

"Lucas…Lucas, could you help me please?" Cyrista was still lying on the ground having trouble getting up with her hands still tied behind her back.

Lucas got up and made his way over to her. He still had the k-bar in his hand so he rolled her over and used it to cut the rope. She jumped to her feet and threw her arms around his neck and kissed him long and hard.

When they broke the kiss, she gave him a puzzled

look and patted him on his chest. She backed up and put both of her hands on his chest. She could see through the hole that the bolt had burned in his shirt that he was wearing something under it.

He was smiling when he lifted his shirt. "It's what Pap-Paw calls an 'edge'. I don't know where he got it, but he gave it to me right before we left the cabin. It's a flack vest, baby. It sure saved my ass, didn't it?"

The Ancient One made his way over to Cyrista and Lucas. He put his big arms around both of them and pulled them close for a hug. "Are you okay, baby girl?" he asked with a tear dripping from his eye.

"I'm fine, Pap-Paw. Nothing could be better now that I've got my two men back in my arms."

They started to walk back toward the bikes and the pickup when they heard Tess crying. She was sitting, holding Terry in her arms and running her fingers through her hair. She looked up at Cyrista, Pap-Paw, and Lucas and said, "You'll pay for this! You'll pay for this."

The old man stopped and gave her a sad look. "We already have paid, little girl. More than you will ever understand."

They went to the bikes and pickup where everyone else was already waiting for them. The whole bunch of them was giving each other hugs and high fives. Most of all, everyone was grateful that none of them were harmed and that they were all together. Gus and Jimmy Legs began loading up the truck with the little bit of gear they had brought.

"Rider," the Ancient One said, "How did you know what to do out there? You played her like you've known her all your life. It was perfect; you just outplayed her, except that first hit you took."

Lucas smiled at the old man and said, "I had a talk with an old friend earlier today; he told me what to do."

Cyrista and Pap-Paw gave each other a puzzled look. They didn't know about his visit to the family cemetery and Lucas wasn't about to tell them.

Gus and Jimmy Legs were sitting in the back of the truck, ready to go. Gus shouted to the others, "Let's go party! I think we've earned it." Everyone laughed and agreed with him.

Cyrista jumped on the back of Lucas's bike. Cissy got on with Bad Billy who reached over and put her little girl up in front of him. Lucas looked back at Cyrista and said, "Looks like Bad Billy will soon be known as Daddy Billy."

Cyrista chuckled and said, "Yeah, it looks that way." She pulled close to Lucas as he and Bad Billy pulled out to lead the way home.

As they pulled out, Lucas looked back to see Terry and Tess sitting alone in the dark on top of the hill. He almost felt sorry for them, but then he thought of the little family cemetery where he had sat earlier that day. Whatever they got, they deserved. He knew that this wouldn't stop them; it would only slow them down for a little while.

They came around a small curve when old Doc started flashing his lights. Lucas and Bad Billy pulled off the road at a small clearing to the side of the road. Everyone dismounted and walked back to where Pap-Paw and Doc were standing beside the pickup with Gus and Jimmy Legs. "What's up?" Lucas asked.

The Ancient One nodded to Gus. Lucas heard two little clicks, and then it happened. All of a sudden there was a hell of a roar and the ground beneath their feet shook and the sky behind them lit up.

No one said a word for a minute; they just looked at each other. The Ancient One looked over to the old Doc and simply said, "Now it's over, Doc."

There was nothing else to be said. Lucas and Cyrista grabbed hands and walked back to the Harley. Lucas noticed that everyone had the same looks on their face except for Cyrista and Pap-Paw. They both looked as if their thoughts were far away; someplace only they could go. He knew they deserved it. They could finally close the book; leave their dead in peace and get on with living their lives for the living and not the dead.

Morning came and Lucas awoke with Cyrista in his arms. The party hadn't lasted long. Cissy was anxious to get home with her little girl. She had been through a lot. She and Bad Billy had a lot to talk about and needed time alone.

Gus and Jimmy knew that they had to get back to work the next morning and could see that everyone else had been pushed to the limit and needed a little quiet time.

Old Doc hadn't even come in. He dropped the others off and headed home. The Ancient One thanked everyone for their help and retired to his room early.

Lucas and Cyrista had to talk. She knew that now that this was over he would be leaving. He asked her to go, even though he knew she couldn't leave Pap-Paw. They left it at that, not wanting to complicate matters. They went to bed and made love, then both slept peacefully.

Lucas got his shower than went out to the porch with a cup of coffee. He looked out over the valley, which had now become a familiar sight, but today, somehow looked different. Lucas didn't give it much thought. He knew after last night that a lot of things would look different.

His heart was heavy. He loved Cyrista and the Ancient One very much. They both wanted him to stay, but he knew he had to get moving. He had to find his own peace. The last few years left him with a lot of unanswered questions. He needed room to find himself.

He rode through the mountains. The thought of Cyrista took control; he could think of nothing else. He had told her he would be back, but he didn't know when. Most other men would never have left. He didn't know exactly why he did, he just knew that if he didn't leave then that he never would. That driving force to keep moving pulled him. If it was meant to be, he would return one day and they could live in peace.